TELEMEDICINE WARS

TELEMEDICINE WARS

G Squared Publishing

****

Historical Fiction

by

MICHAEL GORTON

with contributing authors
Jay H. Sanders, MD
Harvey Castro, MD

••

The stories in this book are all based on real events. The struggles and battles were dramatic and significant.

Had the people involved lacked the absolute determination, the world of access to care would be very different today.

TELEMEDICINE WARS

Cover Graphic Design: Shefa Rumby
Flow Edits * Contributions: Jay H. Sanders, MD
Character Development: Jay H. Sanders, MD & Harvey Castro, MD
Grammar, Flow, & Content Edits: Makenzie Ozycz, MA, MFA
Publicist Lynn McGinnis
G. Byron Brooks for a lifetime of friendship - inspiration
R1b

Michael Gorton, Jay H. Sanders & Harvey Castro.

G Squared Publishing
www.G2-Pub.com
Author contact: mg@mgalcor.com

When Doctor Brooks first suggested the idea of building a telemedicine company while climbing Kilimanjaro in 2000, it seemed like a "cool" idea.

I didn't know who Jay Sanders was, or how long he had persisted in building this amazing idea. I didn't know how much resistance there would be from traditional and mainstream medicine. I had no idea how many sleepless nights we would all experience while believing and fighting for this dream…

A lot of people are *represented* in this book, but the number of characters has been greatly reduced to make the story readable… I know who you all are, and wherever possible, your stories are in the pages of this book.

Without you, we would not have made it to the summit.

The history of telemedicine would not be what it now is, were it not for the brilliance of G. Byron Brooks, who spent a good two years convincing me to help. As a perfect serendipity, Byron's wife Naoko Kono, MD, the Japanese (NASDA) flight surgeon at NASA, helped test and refine the EMRs we built, along with the PA billing system. With all these assets, we created a perfect storm and then survived its potential destruction.

Still, as the old line from the TV show "Dragnet" goes, the stories you're about to read are true. The names have been changed to protect the innocent …and guilty.

ENJOY!

1

Pixel by Pixel

Spartans, traffic jams, and bad ideas…

480 BCE

Leonidas looked out over the town of Sparta with an impossible decision. The relentless Persian Army was seemingly unstoppable. If he trained every man, woman, and child in Sparta, they would still amount to less than a tenth of the trained Persian soldiers. As dawn crept slowly over the landscape where the Eurotas River met the Ionian sea, the scent of brine from the nearby gulf mixed with the obvious fear of impending doom.

Leonidas had not chosen his warriors lightly. He did not seek the young or simply the strong, but only those who had wives and children. Though he set out to win, he knew this battle was not about victory; it was about defiance. His hand-selected 300 Spartans were men prepared not only to fight, but to die, so that the flame of freedom might endure. They would not run, because they knew what would happen if they did. They would stand and fight to the last man, because they were defending what they loved.

When the Persian messengers first arrived in Sparta, they had demanded earth and water, the symbols of submission. Leonidas wouldn't give them either. Instead, he marched north, knowing full well that he was marching toward death. Alongside the 300 came several thousand allies from other Greek city-states, but it was the Spartans who would anchor the line.

The Persian force, led by the Xerxes, numbered somewhere between 300,000 and a million. From the pass at Thermopylae, the Spartans could see an endless tide of humanity stretching beyond the horizon. Their armor gleamed like sunlit rivers. They had so many archers that their arrows would block out the sun, like an ominous thunder cloud. Behind the archers were countless seasoned soldiers who had swarmed and won every battle they had fought. In the ocean behind the soldiers was the largest fleet ever assembled. By every rational measure, Greece was already lost.

Thermopylae, aka: the Hot Gates, was a natural bottleneck. No more than fifty feet wide at its narrowest, it nullified the Persian numerical advantage. There, with bronze shields locked and spears braced, the Greeks waited.

The first day came with waves of Medes and Cissians charging the wall of Spartans. But Leonidas and his 300 fought like men possessed. Their phalanx seemed unbreakable, with discipline forged through decades of brutal training, but sustained mostly by the love they had for their families at home. No strategist or historian could have guessed how the Persian bodies would pile high, creating yet another new obstacle for the invading forces.

On the second day, the Persians sent the Immortals, an elite force cloaked in black that was said to be unbeatable. Yet even they broke upon the shield-wall, their numbers blunted by the sheer fury and precision of Spartan defense.

Xerxes watched from his golden throne, enraged and bewildered. For every attack, the Spartans had an answer. For every foe, a reply carved in muscle, bronze, discipline, and passion to defend their home.

But betrayal would do what brute force could not. A local Greek named Ephialtes, enticed by Persian gold and promises, revealed a hidden mountain trail that flanked the pass. It would allow the Persians to encircle Leonidas and his men.

Warned of this treachery, Leonidas dismissed the bulk of the Greek allies, ordering them to flee and fight another day. He remained with his 300, along with a thousand other Thespians and Thebans.

On the third day, with the sun rising behind Persian standards, Leonidas stood among his warriors; each man knowing this would be their last morning alive. They greeted it not with dread, but with defiant pride.

They had decimated and stopped the mighty Persian Army.

The final battle was chaos and courage incarnate. The Spartans fought with broken spears, then with swords, then with bare hands and teeth. Leonidas fell, pierced by arrows, surrounded by his fallen comrades. Yet the fight did not end. His men rallied around his body, determined that not a single Persian would pass unbloodied.

By nightfall, the Hot Gates were choked with the dead. Xerxes claimed victory, but it was a victory drenched in shame and loss. His own men began to question whether they could stand against another group of Spartans, and they were right. The stand of Leonidas and the 300 did not stop the Persians, but it sparked a fire and confidence in the hearts of all Greeks. Months later, at Salamis and Plataea, the tide would turn. The Persians would retreat. And Greece would remain free.

* * *

1967 - The Summer of Love

It was the kind of Boston day when the city felt like a simmering pot. Tourists were darting here and there in a seemingly aimless chaos of movement, slowing and congesting the already inefficient flow. The humidity was thick enough to fill a swimming pool, and the Red Sox banners fluttered with great intent and hope for a pennant. For the Sox, it would be the year of Carl Yastrzemski.

From the passenger seat of his battered blue Oldsmobile, Dr. Larry

Charles tapped the steering wheel in a syncopated rhythm to the raspy chorus of the Rolling Stones' *Let's Spend the Night Together*, fighting the urge to lay on the horn in the slow-crawling traffic of the Sumner Tunnel.

It was three miles from Logan Airport to Massachusetts General Hospital, he thought. Three miles and an hour of his life, every time, twice a day. Charles glanced at his watch. Another consult was waiting, another patient, and another hospital corridor. If only there were a better way, he thought to himslef.

He cut the radio, the music fading beneath the clamor of engines and distant voices. Sweat dripped down his brow, soaking into the stiff collar of his white shirt.

"Boston traffic is a disease with no cure," Charles muttered, running a hand through his thinning hair.

As the taillights flickered ahead, an idea began to form. "I don't have to be a traffic engineer," he whispered to himself. There were too many variables and not enough time. A better idea then emerged: *Why not bring the hospital to the airport?* Not physically, but virtually. Charles thought about the simple TV sitting in his living room at home. "If I can watch the Sox play the Cardinals, and Cronkite can cross the world with a camera, why can't I use the same technology to cross three-and-a-half painful miles?"

By the time his Oldsmobile emerged from the tunnel, Charles had convinced himself that this crazy idea might just work.

* * *

At Mass General, third-year resident Klark Thomas hovered by the nurses' station, studying a patient file and quietly singing along to The Beatles' song *Yesterday*, which drifted from a nurse's portable radio. "Oh, I believe in yesterday," he stopped mid-verse as Charles busted in, eyes shining.

"Klark!" Charles waved a stack of folders. "I've had a revelation. Traffic is the problem. We're going to solve it."

Klark glanced at the sweat-stained doctor and grinned. "That's ambitious, Dr. Charles. Are you going back to engineering school, or maybe planning to run for mayor?"

Charles leaned in, voice urgent. "I'm serious, Thomas. I waste an hour getting from Logan to the hospital every day. What if we set up a television camera at the airport and another here? We could examine patients, consult with staff, and never even leave MGH!"

Klark raised an eyebrow. "On TV? With black-and-white screens? Are we gonna have someone at each station adjusting rabbit ears?"

Charles ignored the quip. "Think about it, Klark. The tech's good enough for Cronkite, and it made superstars out of the Beatles on Sullivan."

"This's different," Klark started tenuously.

"It's not," Charles responded adamantly. "We could consult and diagnose remotely. This idea could save time and lives."

Klark hesitated, weighing skepticism against the twinkle of genius in Charles's eye. "If you can talk the hospital board into it, I'll scrub in for the first remote appendectomy. But if the screen fizzles during the operation, you're buying lunch for a week."

Charles laughed. "Deal. And we won't start with operations; instead, we'll begin with the basics. Remember one of the fundamentals you were taught in med school: *listen to your patients, and they will tell you what's wrong with them.*"

Klark nodded, trying to paint a convincing smile. In reality, it seemed like the stupidest idea he'd ever heard, particularly coming from a man as respected as Larry Charles. Still, Charles was his boss, and success at Mass General was directly related to Charles's approval.

* * *

Later, Klark tested the idea on Nurse Jennice Walters, who, in her first week, had already proven herself faster than the orderlies and sharp enough to think through most of the problems she had faced. It was, in fact, young nurses like Walters who would shape Dr. Thomas's perspective on the importance and value of nurses in a world where medical doctors often looked down on them.

Over the next six months, the plan came together. Even though there was a bit of pushback at MGH, Charles was a well-respected leader. As such, equipment was purchased, installed, and tested.

Jennice stood at the Logan Airport sickbay, crisp cap perched atop her head, adjusting the clunky video camera as Klark fiddled with the tuning dials on the hospital's end.

"You look nervous, Dr. Thomas," Jennice teased, glancing at her grainy image on the screen. "Is this the first time seeing yourself on TV?"

Klark smirked, his reflection a gray blur on the monitor. "Well, I'm not Doctor Kildare, and this isn't exactly like singing Beatles songs at the nursing station."

Jennice's laughter crackled through the speaker. "My mother doesn't believe in television doctors. She can't look directly in the eye and shake hands with them. Hope you don't mind if I break the news gently."

"Just tell her we come highly pixelated," Klark joked.

* * *

Dr. Paul Castro, the quiet genius behind the hospital's computer project, had spent the last few months silently watching the development from a distance. It wasn't exactly his purview, but the implications were fascinating and, in his view, critical to the future of care. At Mass General, he had been developing the first electronic medical record, but Castro's vision went significantly further than creating a universal storage place for medical records. For him, the computer could someday be used as a tool by doctors in diagnosis and possibly even treatment protocols.

On this day, in December 1967, he stood with his arms crossed watching from the doorway. He envisioned a future where data could save lives once it was organized, accessible, and adequately tested. Paul made a silent note: *Television, remote medicine, and informatics will one day converge.*

Was it serendipity or chance that these seeds had been planted in the same garden in the summer of 1967?

With Charles supervising and Castro observing, Klark and Jennice adjusted the equipment.

* * *

The first patient was a young stewardess with a sprained ankle, grinning nervously as Jennice propped up her foot for the camera.

Through the tiny TV set, Charles's voice was unmistakable. "Tell me what happened, Miss?"

Jennice relayed details, pointing to the swelling and flexing the ankle on command. Klark scribbled notes. The image wasn't perfect, but the diagnosis was fast, effective, and, for the first time, not delayed by Boston's legendary traffic.

Jennice barely had time to log her first remote case before a wiry man in a wrinkled suit shuffled into the exam area, sniffling and dabbing at his nose with a napkin from the airport diner. He looked nervously at the camera, then at the TV screen, before focusing on Nurse Walters, who was smiling and attentive.

"Is this the infirmary?" the man asked tenuously.

Jennice smiled, friendly but professional. "Sir, I'm Nurse Walters. You have the opportunity to speak with one of the finest doctors alive today.

He's located on the other side of the river at Mass General through this television. Please have a seat and tell us what brings you in."

He sniffed, eyes watering. "Just a cold, I think. I have to get to Chicago for a sales meeting. My boss will kill me if I miss this flight, but I'm not feeling well."

Klark, watching on his end, leaned forward so his image filled the tiny screen in Logan's sickbay. "Hi, I'm Dr. Thomas. How long have you had symptoms?"

The man's voice crackled back, "Started yesterday. Stuffy nose, scratchy throat, a bit of a cough. No fever, though."

Dr. Charles, listening in, sat next to Thomas and joined the conversation. "Any body aches or chills? Is anyone else at home sick?"

The patient shook his head. "Just me, I guess. Maybe the winter air got to me."

Jennice pressed a thermometer under his tongue and, after a minute, read it off for the doctors. "99.3."

Dr. Charles considered. "Sir, even a minor cold can be contagious. Flying in a sealed plane, you could share those germs with everyone onboard. I recommend you rest and reschedule your flight. It may be an important meeting, but I recommend you don't risk spreading this to your fellow airline passengers and colleagues in Chicago."

The man's face fell. "Easy for you to say, Doc. My boss isn't on this flight."

Thomas managed a half-grin. "Tell him your doctor ordered it by television medicine. If that doesn't impress him, nothing will. It will be a great story to help you seal that important sale next week. Jennice will give you a note."

Jennice, already writing, winked at the camera. "First 'television sick note' ever issued at Logan Airport."

Charles's eyes gleamed. "And perhaps the first time someone skipped a flight thanks to a Boston traffic jam."

No sooner had they finished when Jennice waved over a harried mother and her young daughter, a six-year-old redhead with a rash spreading across her cheeks and tiny red spots blooming on her arms. Jennice gently helped the girl onto the exam table, adjusting the camera for a better view.

Thomas, on his monitor, caught sight of the rash and felt a chill. "Ma'am, has your daughter been running a fever?"

The mother nodded. "Yes. Starting last night, and she's been fussy all morning. We're supposed to fly home to Minneapolis in an hour."

Dr. Charles thought about it for a second. It was already winter in Boston, so insects, poison ivy, and other similar factors could easily be ruled out. "Did you notice the rash before today?"

Jennice moved the camera closer, letting Charles and Thomas examine the pattern.

Charles looked at Thomas. "Klark, what do you see?"

Klark's tone shifted from skeptical to one of concern. "Ma'am, has your daughter had the measles?"

"Not yet," the mom answered.

"Jennice," Thomas continued, "It appears like a classic measles rash from here. What do you see?"

"Looks like measles to me, Doctor Thomas," Walters nodded.

Charles felt like a broken record as he realized that we would be responsible for canceling the flights for two of the first three patients. "Ma'am, I know this is inconvenient, but your daughter shouldn't board that flight. The measles is contagious, and she could spread it to everyone on that plane who hasn't had it. We'll help you get treatment here."

The mother blinked away tears, relief and fear mingling on her face. "Thank you, doctors. Having her get better is far more important than the trip."

Jennice handed the girl a lollipop, whispering, "You're the bravest patient at Logan today."

As the connection faded, Klark leaned back in his chair, a strange exhilaration welling up inside him. He'd started this project because he felt forced to do so, thinking Charles's idea was another distraction in a world that already seemed overwhelming. But here, right now, he saw the future. This tool not only delivered faster consultations but also had a real public health impact. A chain of infections had broken before they even began. Lives quietly saved in transit.

He looked over at Charles, who wore a small, knowing smile.

"Okay, Dr. Charles, I get it," Klark said quietly. "This isn't just about moving faster or dodging traffic. It's about connecting care where it matters when it matters, about stopping an outbreak before it even starts. In addition, it's about being a true front line for patients, wherever they are."

Charles nodded. "That's the idea, Klark."

We ended the summer thinking the Sox were going to win the Pennant, but even with Yaz, we got eliminated. Still, that's not the story of the year. Thomas stared at the screen, watching Jennice cradle the girl's hand and comfort her mother. His mind spun with possibilities.

"Remote television medicine, Klark. It's the future," Charles motioned at the screen.

At that point, Dr. Castro stepped into the room, "Doctors," he greeted them politely.

"Doctor Castro," Thomas stood and acknowledged him.

"The word television comes from the Latin word tele, which means far away," Castro added. "So, it means vision from far away. Kind of like watching Cronkite from the Washington bureau while we are here in Boston."

"Makes sense." The beginnings of the term telemedicine were shaping in Charles's head.

"We don't even have a real specialty for this," Thomas broke in. "What we are mostly doing in the ER. What we have done here today. We are the first point of contact, generalists who see everything and everyone. Maybe that's what we need. A new kind of specialty that focuses on primary care. This television medicine should be a primary tool in delivery, how we get there."

Charles's smile grew. "Well, Klark, maybe you just found your calling."

* * *

The break room at Mass General wasn't much more than a converted closet with a coffee maker, a metal table, and chairs that creaked every time someone sat or shifted their weight. The fluorescent lights flickered and buzzed overhead like oversized house flies. Some of the staff stayed away, others relaxed, thriving on the chaos.

It was later than anyone decent should be working, but Klark Thomas sat slouched in the corner chair, tie loosened, white coat unbuttoned, with a cup of stale coffee steaming in his hand, oblivious to the neon assault above his head.

He stared at the corkboard on the wall, cluttered with posters about infection control, CPR refreshers, and one suspiciously yellowed memo about "coffee rationing." But he wasn't *really* looking at any of it.

"Television medicine." He muttered and exhaled hard.

Of all the things he'd hoped to do during residency, practicing medicine between television sets and cameras was not one of them. A few months ago, he would have thought more about publishing, teaching, or maybe landing a fellowship at Columbia or Miami. Nothing in his wildest imagination could've led to this project, which consisted of babysitting a clunky tube monitor and adjusting dials like a stagehand at a public access studio.

He muttered aloud, "I didn't go to med school to play engineer or cameraman."

Just then, the door creaked open. Jennice Walters stepped in, carrying a clipboard, a smile, and her usual air of quiet confidence. Her cap sat slightly askew, the only hint that she'd been running hard all day.

"Do you always talk to yourself in the haunted breakroom this late at night, Dr. Thomas?" she asked with a teasing smile.

"Haunted?" he asked.

"Building maintenance could probably fix it," she pointed up at the neon lights. "Every time I come in here, I always have to double check to make sure I'm not under attack by some angry hornets."

"It keeps the crowds out, Miss Walters," Klark straightened in his chair but didn't try to mask his exhaustion. "Anyway, I only talk to myself when I'm trying to convince myself not to run away and open a jazz bar in New Orleans or go work at Regina's Pizzeria."

She laughed. "That's oddly specific."

"Isn't it?" He took a sip. "Wouldn't need to worry about cross-coverage protocols or whether the camera's pointed at someone's elbow instead of their face."

Jennice walked over to the counter and poured herself a cup, black. She leaned back against the counter, watching him over the rim. "You don't like this project, do you?"

Klark shook his head slowly. "I am doing it because I'm smart enough to not buck my professor, but I constantly have to ask myself whether it really is medicine. I had other plans as I was finishing my residency, but mostly, I just keep asking myself if the world of medicine is really ready for this."

She sipped her coffee, then set the cup down with care. The chair squeaked. "I hate these chairs almost as much as those neon lights."

Klark chuckled and focused on her.

"More importantly," she started thoughtfully. "I see your perspective, Doctor Thomas, but have you considered the possibility that maybe you're too close to see the full picture?"

"Oh? And what picture is that?"

"That you're not diagnosing a rash through a camera. You're opening a door that's been closed to a lot of people. People who don't have the privilege to be five blocks from Mass General. People who can't afford to miss work or sit in traffic while their fever spikes."

Klark looked at her, surprised. "You sound like you've given this a lot of thought."

"I have," she said, tilting her head. "My mom's diabetic. She lives in a rural county in Vermont. Nearest doctor is fifty miles away on winding mountain roads. She missed an appointment two years ago and ended up in the ER with an infection."

He let that sink in.

"I get it," she added more softly. "You didn't sign up to be the poster boy for a box with wires and dials. You are a brilliant doctor, but maybe, just maybe, you're the only *person* who can get it right."

Something about her comments and delivery made Klark focus more intently than he had in the past. Since starting med school, he had been undistracted and singularly focused on a goal. Suddenly, he was having a conversation with a woman. She had a strong jawline and eyes too intelligent to ever be ignored. Something in her voice softened when she talked about her mother. He found himself smiling, feeling something non-clinical and long forgotten, despite his fatigue.

"I am a fan of the nursing staff. Unlike most doctors, I appreciate your value, but you're smarter than most of the attendings," he said.

"You just figuring that out now?" Jennice winked playfully.

He chuckled. "Maybe. Or maybe I was too busy trying not to notice that you're also… well, incredibly attractive."

She raised an eyebrow but didn't look away. "Does that line work on the other nurses?"

Honestly?" he shrugged. "I haven't tried it on anyone. The last few years, I have been too busy to even notice."

Jennice picked up her coffee again and walked toward the door. "Well, you have an amazing heart, and passion for what you do. That is so very attractive…" she stopped, reconsidering her position. "It's just, well, you know." She ended, tongue tied.

"Thanks, Ms. Walters," Klark nodded with a grin.

"Please, call me Jennice when we're off duty."

When he didn't respond, she stood and walked toward the door. As she opened the door, she paused and glanced back at him.

"Don't run off to New Orleans just yet, Dr. Thomas. I think something important is about to happen here." She winked, smiled, then flicked her brunette hair before leaving the room.

Klark stared at the closed door for a moment, a slow smile curling at the corner of his lips. *What exactly just happened here?*

Maybe the monitor wasn't the only thing flickering to life.

As the quiet hours after midnight settled over Boston and the last notes of Aretha Franklin's *Respect* faded from the airport speakers, a revolution quietly advanced. It began with one sick note, one diagnosis, and one bold new idea at a time.

Despite Yastrzemski's best year, the city endured another season of the Curse of the Bambino. Silently, a new revolution had begun, one that would ultimately change everything. In a windowless room at Mass General, connected to another windowless room at Logan, a city hummed to Motown and licked its World Series wounds, unaware of a revolution in medicine that, pixel by pixel, had just flickered to life.

2

Three Decades of Resistance

Planting seeds

The Second Experiment (1968-1974)

For young Dr. Klark Thomas, Nurse Walters' "pep talk" had a lasting impact. After standing back, he recognized the innovation and possibilities to truly change care delivery. He transitioned from frustration to an affinity for flickering images, and that created a permanent bond which would continue to grow with time. The "Tele-Clinic," as Charles had dubbed it, logged another 312 consultations from Logan by the end of its first full year, each one a small victory against the tyranny of distance and Boston traffic, and remarkably, without a single reported misdiagnosis.

Inside MGH, the project was viewed as niche, but successful. Outside Boston, the ripples were almost nonexistent. Klark Thomas moved on from MGH to a major university hospital system in Florida and became a custodian of the technology. He swapped out the bulky, heat-radiating tube monitors for sleeker Sony Trinitrons that used color images. By 1974, Klark transmitted an otoscope image in under two seconds—a minor miracle of modern engineering that still managed to impress only the occasional intrigued reporter or visiting dignitary looking for a glimpse of "the future."

Unfortunately, the brief, but intense spark between he and Nurse Walters had not evolved. She had given him ample opportunities, but the timing was never right for Klark Thomas. When he moved to Florida, that link broke.

Klark decided to pitch a telemedicine project to a skeptical hospital administrator during a 1973 budget review. The University of Florida's Medical Sciences Building was a fortress of traditional decision making surrounded by concrete and bureaucracy. Klark Thomas, now two years removed from Boston, stood in a second-floor conference room outfitted with a chalk board, a flickering fluorescent panel, and a speakerphone with a mind of its own.

Across from him sat Senior Associate Dean of Clinical Advancement, and, more importantly, the gatekeeper of the school's annual technology budget.

Johnson was in his late forties and had spent his entire career in medicine, beginning with medical school at University of Florida. He always wore a crisp suit, seamlessly knotted tie, and perfectly polished shoes. He was a traditionalist who didn't suffer fools but clearly had taken an interest in the potential for telemedicine.

Klark took a deep breath and handed a stapled presentation with 14 sheets of paper to Doctor Johnson.

"Have a look at page five," he said. "This graph shows a 31% decrease in ER visit load across pilot sites where telemedicine protocols were used for triage. Page six shows a side-by-side comparison of a patient case managed remotely versus traditional in-person care. Our calculus shows nearly $400 savings per encounter."

Johnson nodded slowly. "You're advocating for the ER, to adopt a virtual care model?"

"Yes, sir. A structured one. With protocols, screening, and a secure communication backbone. I suggest we start with one clinic that has two video stations."

Johnson interlocked his fingers and leaned back. "Let me ask you something, Dr. Thomas. What do we do when the connection drops mid-consult? Or the resolution's too poor to catch a subtle rash? What happens when a lawyer asks us under cross examination why we didn't bring the patient in?"

Klark anticipated the resistance. "Fair concerns, but I think we can agree that every tool has limits. The role of telemedicine is not to replace physical medicine, but to expand access. If we treat the right cases remotely, we *free up* in-person resources for the complex ones. Harvard and Mass General are doing it. I believe The University of Florida can leap ahead and set the gold standard."

Johnson studied him for a moment, then flipped through a tabbed document. "You're clearly passionate and your proposal is thorough. What you are suggesting is conservative on costs and seems to properly assess the risk."

Klark allowed himself a flicker of hope.

"But," Johnson said, voice soft but resolute, "the Cardiovascular Research Division just submitted a competing request. They want to build an engine that has a couple of donors interested. The Board sees that as a strategic growth area."

Klark blinked. "So, telemedicine gets shelved?"

Johnson didn't smile, but he wasn't unkind. "Deferred. For now. Let's call it a matter of timing. Cardiovascular advances bring prestige. Heart transplants are cool and, well, mainstream. It garners high-profile publications and headlines. What you're proposing is revolutionary, but also controversial."

Klark exhaled and nodded. He'd heard this before. Quiet revolutions didn't fundraise well.

Johnson closed the folder and stood. "I appreciate your effort, Dr. Thomas. Don't stop pushing. Just understand that medicine isn't always driven by logic. It's driven by what donors can understand, and sometimes, what the front page will print."

Klark shook his hand, said his thanks, and left the room.

As the door clicked shut behind him, he muttered under his breath, "Quiet revolutions still change the world." So, with a sigh and a suitcase full of ideas, Klark decided to take his show on the road.

Doctor Thomas pressed on, pitching the idea to fifteen yawning residents at the University of North Carolina. Most were too tired from their 24-hour shifts to even process the new idea.

A distinguished surgery professor with arms crossed barked from the back row after Klark demonstrated a remote skin lesion examination, "Son, if I can't palpate the abdomen, and can't feel the turgor of the skin with my own damn hands, I can't rightly call it medicine!"

Dismissive laughter followed Klark out of the auditorium.

"We have seen thousands of patients using telemedicine, sir," Dr. Thomas responded politely. "We are almost always able to resolve the issue."

"This is not real medicine, and I am surprised that this quackery originated at an institution as respected as MGH and Harvard," the professor scanned the group of residents, making sure to catch their eyes, then turned and walked out of the room.

Klark nodded silently as he watched the students leave the room, one by one.

Two years later, Dr. Thomas was working with a team in Madison, Wisconsin. Approval seemed imminent when a blizzard howled outside, the wind chill plummeting to a bone-aching –40°F. Inside, the university's aging electrical system chose that moment to stage a protest. A modem connecting to a remote clinic broke connection, re-dialed, and failed to connect. Decision makers stood patiently while the tech unsuccessfully tried to reconnect. There was no grant issued, and the idea quickly died for that system in an apparent stroke of proof for its opponents.

In a 1979 Berkely project, students in the tech-savvy Bay Area cheered the innovation. The dean, however; a man whose spectacles seemed permanently perched on the edge of skepticism slid Klark a brochure titled *Malpractice in the Video Age: A Primer for the Unwary Innovator.* Another polite but firm rejection.

Dr. Thomas remained stalwart through every campus visit and every rejection, each time adding a layer of refinement. Stanford's engineers demonstrated advancements in low-light camera technology. MIT's early computer scientists introduced the concept of packetized still-frames for clearer image transmission over noisy lines. Georgia Tech had a rudimentary touch-tone scheduling system that sparked ideas. The system matured in the crucible of rejection, becoming leaner, more robust, and more *possible.*

The breakthroughs, when they came, were not in the hallowed halls of academia but in the pragmatic, problem-solving corners of society.

* * *

In 1983, a violent riot at Laurel Highlands Correctional Facility left two medical interns seriously injured and the prison's administration desperate. The risk officers at Penn State, having heard a whisper of Klark's work, made a hesitant call. Within three months, a sturdy 19-inch television monitor, encased in bullet-proof Lexan, sat in the prison infirmary. Inmates, initially wary, soon dubbed it *"the magic window.*" Assaults on medical staff during consultations dropped by a staggering 70% in the first year.

It seemed that an avenue for the introduction of telemedicine had found itself in a prison! For Klark, this was the first real opportunity that seemed to make sense. Still, what he wanted was a mainstream avenue that would bring telemedicine to the masses.

In 1986 a devastating drought seared the Midwest cornfields. Heat-stroke cases soared, and the stoic farming community saw a heartbreaking rise in stress-related illnesses and suicides. The University of Iowa, seeking any solution, agreed to wire four rural county clinics to its main hospital in Iowa City, using Klark's now well-honed protocols. Farmers whose workloads preempted the long farm to city drive for care, parked their dusty tractors beside makeshift antenna masts at local coops and engaged in video consults. State agricultural insurance payouts for preventable health crises fell by 20%. Klark, for the first time, tasted widespread, measurable success—regional, humble, but undeniably honest.

* * *

Everything began to change in the 1990s, when the State of Texas granted inmates the right to see a doctor within 24 hours of a request. Initially, the solution was a combination of bringing providers into the secure areas of a correctional facility or transporting inmates out for care. Neither approach was ideal.

Klark Thomas was invited to speak at the UT Medical Branch in Galveston. Sitting in the audience was Byron Cook, a seasoned electrical engineer who had also attended medical school and was serving as a flight surgeon at both NASA and UTMB. Cook listened intently to the lecture, took notes, and watched the resistance from his colleagues. Dr. Cook was not aware of how long Thomas had been dealing with telemedicine pushbacks, but admired his calm and confident response to the negative reactions.

At the end of the lecture, without asking any questions, Cook got up and left. While his colleagues were using the Q&A to ridicule and question efficacy, Cook felt inspired. That evening, he thought about this "new" telemedicine methodology. As an MD and flight surgeon who had been treating astronauts in space, he had clarity on remote care. And as an engineer who had done a stint in telecom, he also understood the technology and connectivity required to make it work.

Cook's approach to medicine was rooted in methodical precision and an unshakeable belief in data. For him, the telemedicine approach grew from mild consideration to passion. He began to design a network of secure video carts, cameras, and monitors that could be installed in examination rooms within the prison system. The guards appreciated the increased safety, and the doctors were relieved to remain unharmed. For the first time, the state mandate of delivering care withing 24-hours was consistently able to be met.

* * *

On a spring morning in 1997, Klark Thomas woke in one of the many hotels he had endured over the twenty years since his professor, Larry Charles, had first introduced the idea of telemedicine. He rolled out of bed and thought, *What city am I in again?*

He showered, shaved, then remembered: today was Johns Hopkins. He packed his bag, flipped through the slides he had presented hundreds of times before, then headed to the auditorium.

The room was packed with faculty and eager medical students. Klark was on slide twelve, detailing the Iowa Tele-Farm Network's success metrics, when a voice cut through the room. It was the first interruption. Klark turned off the overhead projector and studied the sharp, confident, youthful student who beamed with arrogance.

"Dr. Thomas, with all due respect, how precisely do you propose to take an accurate blood pressure through a cathode-ray tube?"

Klark, accustomed to such questions, replied calmly, "We utilize patient-operated cuffs, often guided by a nurse or technician on-site, and increasingly, digital stethoscopes that can transmit sounds clearly and accurately."

"So," the student continued with a confident smirk, "you're essentially outsourcing the physician's hands, our most fundamental diagnostic tools, to amateurs, to nurses and technicians, or worse, to the patient themself?"

A ripple of chuckles went through the faculty section. Klark glanced at the student's name tag: B. Crane. He mentally filed the name away. "I do not consider nurses and technicians to be amateurs, Doctor Crane. Furthermore, I believe your best professors in this medical school will attest to the fact that the best data on a patient's condition often comes from that patient's own words."

"I beg to differ, Mister Thomas," Crane started

"It's Doctor Thomas, if you please," Klark interrupted.

"Right, well, Doctor Thomas, technicians and nurses are fine, but they are not trained to the level that we are."

"Your position is noted, Doctor Crane," Thomas responded in a cool, confident tone. "Anything else?"

"Nope," Crane winked confidently at one of his colleagues, then at his professor, and took his seat. A part of him felt like he had just fought an important battle in a war he knew his side would win.

After the lecture, as Klark was attempting to pour himself a cup of lukewarm coffee, he was cornered by that professor, Dr. Victor Malor, the distinguished, silver-haired chair of Pathophysiology. Malor's smile was smooth, almost silky.

"That was an interesting presentation, Dr. Thomas. You sell hope and a compelling narrative of access, but hope, doctor, is a fragile commodity. Medicine, true medicine, requires certainty, the tangible. The laying on of hands."

Klark shrugged in the friendliest way possible. "And yet, we have two decades of data that says otherwise."

"Perhaps I wasn't clear, Doctor Thomas," Malor said, frowning and shaking his head in a condescending manner. "This is not medicine. It's not what I teach in my classes. And if I have anything to say about it, you will never take this beyond your quaint little experiments. Doctors heal by being present, by touching and feeling the room. The practice of medicine will not tolerate your technological laziness and voodoo connectivity. You can count me as a vocal opponent who will do everything in my power to make sure your dangerous telemedicine game ends before people start dying."

"Thank you for your time, sir," Klark said. He had been in this position many times over the years and had learned that it was better to bow out gracefully than to debate.

Klark drove to Baltimore-Washington International Airport that evening, Malor's condescending words and the image of the smug student, Crane, echoing in his mind. The weight of years of polite dismissals felt heavier than usual. It was time to pay a visit to his mentor, Larry Charles.

* * *

It was late afternoon when Klark Thomas pulled into the familiar gravel driveway of a modest colonial tucked into the outskirts of Cambridge. The same windchimes that used to greet him during medical school visits had survived the decades and were dancing lightly in the breeze.

Klark stepped up on the porch and knocked.

The door creaked open. "Klark?" came the unmistakable baritone of Dr. Charles, now wrinkled, frail, and bald. He moved more slowly, but was still more alert than most people half his age.

"Afternoon, sir."

Charles smiled. "You're still formal. I like that." He opened the door. "Come in. You want coffee or something harder?"

"Coffee's fine, sir."

They settled into the backyard garden. The rhododendrons were blooming. A bird feeder swayed lazily in the corner. During the time he was a resident, Klark enjoyed the relaxing nature of this home, which now seemed a perfect location for retirement.

Klark sipped the coffee. It was hot, but far too strong for his liking. He smiled, took a second sip, and cut to the point. "I need help."

Charles leaned back, his expression unreadable. "Okay son, what can I do for you?"

"It's been 30 years, professor. Telemedicine is making small steps, but the resistance from mainstream medicine has been nonstop. I've pitched hospital administrators, state universities, and even a couple of venture groups. They all nod and smile and then invest in shiny machines and cardiology labs. I'm running out of doors to knock on."

Charles stared into his cup, swirling it slightly. "I read the article on your Iowa pilot. Impressive numbers."

"That was an anomaly," Klark admitted. "The rural clinic director lost his brother to heat stroke and wanted to make a difference. But outside those stories, I can't get traction. No one wants to champion something this… invisible."

Charles nodded slowly. "Because it's not glamorous. No headlines. No cocktail parties with donors. Just quiet impact."

"That's the thing, sir," Klark answered with a tight voice. "The results have always been impactful. And you're the one who made me see that."

Charles gave a soft chuckle. "Yes, but I also told you the world doesn't move just because something works. It moves when the right people believe it should."

Klark leaned forward, hopeful. "I've dedicated my life to this work, professor, and I feel like I'm still at or near the starting line. Can you think of a way to help me evangelize this? Let's do what we did at Logan. We convinced everyone at Harvard and Mass General. Can we find a way to pull some of those old MGH strings, but do it on a national level?"

Charles set down his cup and looked off toward the tree line. For a long moment, he didn't answer.

Finally, he spoke. "Klark… I'm proud of you. I truly am. You've taken something fragile and carried it further than I ever expected it to go. But I'm in my late 70s. My life has transformed to geriatrics and grandkids who think I'm Santa Claus. I no longer have the energy or influence. I've moved on."

Klark tried not to show the sting. "So, that's it?"

Charles looked him in the eye. "That's not *it*. You've been the evangelist, and you've planted seeds all over the country, hell, all over the world. I suspect the big break is coming, and soon."

The words hung in the garden like dew.

"You don't need me to convince people," Charles added gently. "You're sharper than I ever was, and you've seen more use cases in five years than I saw in twenty. But this is your crusade now. In truth, it has always been your crusade."

Klark stared into his empty cup, then nodded. "Understood."

Charles smiled and clapped him on the shoulder. "You're doing something important. Don't let the silence convince you otherwise."

"It's not the silence that keeps me up at night, sir, it's the resistance."

"Tell me about that, Klark."

"Do you happen to know Victor Malor?"

"Unfortunately, yes. Is he one of the protagonists?"

"He's the worst yet," Klark responded, still feeling the sting.

"I suspect we'd still be bleeding patients if he had real power. Ignore him, son. He's mostly just a big mouth. A brilliant one, but just big."

"Okay." Klark stood and shook his mentor's hand.

"Look, Klark, I can see that this has been tough, but I can also see the progress you've made. The other thing I can tell you for sure is that your passion has not diminished. You are disappointed with the progress, but I am certain, in the end, you will win."

Klark realized Doctor Charles was right. Inside him was a smoldering fire, but what Professor Chales had just done was finally fully pass the torch. Up until now, his role had just been one of Charles' torch bearers. Now, the torch was his.

The passing of the torch wasn't loud. It was quiet, like most revolutions. But it had happened.

He got in his car, the sun dipping low on the Boston horizon, and whispered to himself as he pulled out of the driveway: "All right then. Let's make some noise."

Two weeks later, an invitation to a University of Texas Medical Branch symposium on "Innovations in Healthcare Delivery" landed on Klark's desk. He nearly threw it away. The thought of facing another skeptical audience and having to explain the obvious again was exhausting. But something, perhaps the stubborn refusal to let Malor and Crane have the last word, made him book the flight to Galveston anyways.

Mostly, Klark Thomas wanted to test his new torch.

A fierce Gulf storm was brewing as Klark took the podium, the auditorium windows rattling with each gust of wind. Whether it was the storm or his renewed determination, Klark delivered his leanest, most direct pitch yet: twelve slides, no jokes, just unvarnished data and undeniable potential.

In the third row sat Dr. Byron Cook, an attentive medical doctor and electrical engineer, exuding an air of quiet intensity. After the applause died down, Cook approached the podium, his questions precise, almost mathematical.

For a moment, Thomas thought this had to be the last time. He was done presenting to mean-spirited physicians with god-complexes and determination that telemedicine should be outlawed. Twenty years ago, it seemed like a great idea, one that produced nothing but positive results. Now, the resistance felt endless.

By the time he was at the end of his questions, most of the audience had dissipated. Cook stood, and started to turn away, but changed his mind and faced Klark squarely. "Dr. Thomas, impressive data from Iowa and Pennsylvania. I estimate an eighty-seven-percent feasibility for a broader application with a structured Electronic Medical Record. The video interface adds perhaps another five percent of diagnostic confidence in select cases."

"I'm sorry, who are you again?" Thomas asked.

Cook stuck his hand out, shook Klark's, and responded, "I'm Byron Cook. I did my residency as a flight surgeon, and I love what you've been doing."

Thomas fought back a tear. "Thank you, Doctor Cook. I'm not accustomed to physicians agreeing that telemedicine is a good idea."

"Right, I gathered that," Cook smiled. "Screw them. Anyway, I was at your last lecture here, and because of that lecture, I've implemented a system for correctional care here in Texas. It's working well."

"That's good to hear, Doctor Cook."

"Why don't you help me scale it for the general population?"

"The general population?" Klark glanced out at the rain-lashed windows, the memory of Crane's skepticism still fresh. "How would you do that?" He asked, with a bit of skepticism in his voice.

"Take it straight to the patients. As an engineer and MD, I have learned that doctors are not technical. We have to keep it simple for starters. I think we should remove the video component, for now, at least."

"Doctor Cook, it's not telemedicine if we eliminate the television," Klark protested.

"Check your data, Doctor Thomas. Mine shows that we can treat about 80% of the calls with a doctor, a medical history, a patient, and a telephone."

"Dr. Cook, I appreciate that. But I'm tired of fighting practically everyone in the established medical community just to incorporate video. I cannot even imagine what that battle would be like without it."

"I have tested it, Doctor Thomas, and it works," Cook took a deep breath and exhaled with a slow confidence. "Simplicity is the best pathway to success."

"If the future isn't seen, meaning if we can't incorporate reliable video, I'm not sure that I'm your man."

"Then let's look at ways to ensure the cameras are wired and the bandwidth is sufficient. Coffee tomorrow morning? My treat."

Klark Thomas, feeling a flicker of hope he hadn't realized was so diminished, agreed. The storm outside raged on, but inside, a new current was forming.

* * *

The convention center in San Diego buzzed with energy. Klark slipped past the vendor booths with practiced indifference, skimming the room for familiar faces and dodging product demos like landmines. He'd just finished moderating a panel on "Telemedicine and the Next Decade," and all he wanted now was a drink and a quiet table to process the bureaucratic minefield he'd just navigated.

Then he saw her.

Standing beside a kiosk for ultrasound technology, Nurse Jennice Walters was flipping through a conference pamphlet, her brown hair pulled into a no-nonsense bun that somehow made her look more elegant than the last time he saw her. Klark had to stop for a minute and count, was it thirty years ago now?

Klark stared. She had aged a bit, but something about her was different. She hadn't noticed him yet, so he stepped up and cleared his throat.

"Excuse me, ma'am, I think you may have given me the wrong dosage of nostalgia."

She turned slowly. Her eyes widened. "Klark?"

He smiled. "Nurse Walters," he hugged her. "It's been a few decades."

She laughed with a bright, familiar sound. "Klark Thomas. I didn't know you still did these things."

"Honestly, I usually don't. Got roped into a keynote. What about you? What are *you* doing here? I thought you vanished into suburban sainthood after you left the hospital."

"I went to medical school, so for the record, I am now both Nurse *and*

Doctor Walters," she said, folding her arms with a smirk. "After residency, I married, moved to Houston, and raised three kids. Primary care practice, soccer mom, PTA, the whole cliché. But I kept my license active, took night classes. Guess what?"

"You're running for Congress?"

She chuckled. "Close. I went back to med school, then did my residency in internal medicine. Now I split my time between clinical care and mentoring. And," she added with a little proud grin, "my oldest daughter is doing her residency at Southwestern."

Klark let out a long, low whistle. "That's incredible. Truly. You're a doctor, and your daughter is as well!"

"Took me long enough," she said, brushing a strand of hair behind her ear. "I still remember our conversation that late night in the break room. You called telemedicine a distraction, and I told you it was the future."

Klark nodded. "And I was wrong. At least, I think I was wrong."

"I kept watching," she said gently. "You ended up leading the charge."

For a second, Klark wasn't sure what to say. His mouth opened, then closed again. Finally, he offered, "You want to grab a drink? See if we can compress the last thirty years in less than three hours?"

Walters tilted her head. "You buying?"

"I would be honored to."

They found a quiet bistro tucked along the marina, away from the crowd. Over wine and sea bass, they swapped memories—the old staff lounge, the telemed pilot, and the angry neon lights that drove people out of the break room. Walters laughed until she cried.

"So," Klark asked carefully, "Tell me about your husband…how's married life these days?"

Her smile faltered just enough to be honest. "Divorced. Three years ago. Friendly, but final."

"I'm sorry."

She shrugged, the way people do when they've made peace with disappointment. "We grew in different directions. Happens."

Klark raised his glass. "To second acts."

"To third and fourth ones too," she added, clinking his glass.

By dessert, the conversation turned back to the future—hers, his, and maybe even something shared between the two. There were sparks again, but gentler this time. Grown-up sparks. The kind that knew life was short, but still left room for old connections to bloom.

3

The Digital & Healthcare Courtship

Mass General - Boston

It was late 1994 when, wearing an ear-to-ear grin, Dr. Ray Kurtz proudly wheeled a beige tower PC into the physician's lounge. With an almost evangelical gleam in his eye, he declared, "Gentlemen and ladies, meet Chronos, the electronic memory you never knew you needed but soon won't be able to live without."

Dolores Garcia, a recently minted cardiologist stepped up, "What is this contraption, Ray?"

Kurtz, a protégé of the visionary Dr. Paul Castro, had absorbed Castro's lectures on computer-aided diagnostics and recognized the untapped potential of computers and informatics. He'd then spent two caffeine-soaked, sleep-deprived years meticulously coding what would become the hospital's first truly end-to-end Electronic Medical Record (EMR).

But today wasn't about that, it was about the machine that could host it.

Ray studied Dolores, possibly the brightest colleague amongst a group of the best and most elite. "This, my dear friend, is a state-of-the-art Pentium 486 running at 100 megahertz. It has a 500-megabyte hard drive and 16 megabytes of RAM."

"That means nothing to me, Ray," Doctor Garcia interrupted. "Tell me what it can do for me. How will this *megahertz* thing make my job better?"

"Right, right…Chronos," he boasted changing tack, "is a true electronic medical record that can pull lab results in four seconds, cross-check medication interactions against a patient's known allergies, and, the miracle of all miracles, print legible discharge orders."

"Uh huh," Dolores responded. "You just need me to replace my stethoscope with a keyboard?"

"Well, not your stethoscope," Doctor Kurtz responded, placing his hand on the computer as if it were a shrine. "This baby will replace that frustrating file cabinet where you store the patient's medical records."

Dolores Garcia was nearly convinced and about to say so when one of her professors, a senior cardiologist whose scrawl was legendary for its indecipherability, barked, "I prefer my damn handwriting, son. Been doing it for thirty years!"

Right after that, a senior endocrinologist renowned for her meticulous and voluminous paper charts folded her arms. "We all know how often our PCs crash, and when that Chronos contraption inevitably crashes, Doctor Kurtz, blood sugar levels don't politely pause for a reboot."

Ray had prepared for exactly this kind of response under Dr. Castro's mentoring and countered not with rhetoric but with data. "A pilot ward using Chronos had cut charting time by an average of 31% and slashed calls for lost lab results to virtually zero. More importantly, I can instantly make a patient's medical record available anywhere, at any time."

From the doorway, Paul Castro offered a discreet wink, letting his protégé navigate the treacherous waters of medical skepticism on his own.

"We can already move a patient's record anywhere, any time with our fax machine, Doctor Kurtz," the endocrinologist argued. "Furthermore, it seems to me that the computer data is not secure like an old-fashioned file cabinet, safely locked in a hospital."

Kurtz looked at Castro and thought for a second how he would handle this. Dr. Castro had spent years dealing with pushback like this and had learned that argument typically only created animosity. He turned to the endocrinologist, "Of course you are right, Doctor. I would love the opportunity to collaborate with you on how to improve a system like Chronos so we can improve quality of care."

By 1997, nearly a quarter of the hospital staff—reluctant but proficient—were typing into Chronos. By 2000, that number had grown to half, while the stubborn remainder still dictated their notes onto micro-cassettes, which Ray, with a sigh, often digitized himself at night to maintain the integrity of the hospital-wide database.

It was during one of these late-night sessions in late 2000 that a visiting physician from Texas, Byron Cook, who was in Boston for CME, swung by the IT lab to see "the famous computer chart he'd heard whispers about."

Ray, ever the evangelist, eagerly demoed a live pulmonology note, showing how Chronos auto-flagged a critical penicillin allergy just as a junior doctor was about to prescribe an amoxicillin derivative.

Cook was whistling softly, genuinely impressed. "If that EMR can consistently keep me from missing penicillin anaphylaxis, then I would love to see how we can deploy in on a project in Texas, Dr. Kurtz."

They talked late into the night, two innovators recognizing a kindred spirit. They traded email addresses, a novelty (for physicians) at the time. When Cook left Boston to return to Texas, his parting note to Ray read: *Brilliant work. If you ever want to wire the world outside these hallowed but sometimes stifling walls, call me.*

* * *

In the summer of 2001, Ray Kurtz, Klark Thomas, and Byron Cook gathered in a Barnes & Noble coffee shop at 1 NASA Road, just west of Mission Control in Texas. Also in attendance was Cook's boss, an astronaut-MD and telemedicine advocate, Bernard West. Doctor West spent the first hour with the group then told Cook he would cover for him, and help in any way, but would not take a formal role in the new company.

Klark Thomas advocated video as the primary medium, but Cook felt like the complications with delivering video would significantly hamper the efforts to take this service to the masses. After some debate, Doctor Thomas bowed out, and only Cook and Kurtz remained.

When Thomas left, Cook looked at Kurtz, "What do you think about Cyber Medical Services for the name?"

"Are you serious, Byron?" Kurtz immediately hated the name for more reasons than he wanted to state.

"Why? I like the name," Cook argued, crossing his arms and leaning confidently back in his chair.

"First of all, most people won't even know what it means, and second," Kurtz took a deep breath and exhaled slowly, "the name reminds me of the *Terminator* movies. We don't need any more resistance that we already have."

"And your suggestion is…" Cook asked.

"How about something simple, like Television Doc or Telephone Doc, or a shortened version like TeleDoc, or TelaDoc?" Kurtz suggested.

Byron Cook nodded, "I do like those shortened names, but I don't want to confuse people about television. How about something like VirtuCare?"

"That's it!" Ray Kurtz clapped his hands and stood up. "I love the double entendre in the name. VirtuCare, it is."

In January 2002, Byron Cook and Ray Kurtz filed articles of

incorporation for VirtuCare, Inc. The first hundred test patients came to the service through personal phone calls from the two founders. In the first six months, those hundred patients amounted to just under 200 calls, a small but effective number for the company to tweak the model on a daily basis. All of those calls were handled, free of charge, by either Doctor Cook, or Doctor Kurtz. The cases were unglamorous, consisting of coughs, rashes, and worried parents of feverish children, but the underlying promise felt electric. VirtuCare was, quite literally, wiring a new pathway for access to top tier physicians ready to provide care.

By the end of summer 2002, the fledgling service was ready to go public. The 100 test patients all brought in a few friends, and a website was built to help get the word out. A dozen doctors were added to the service and the company started to see real customers willing to pay a nice fee for this new level of access to care.

* * *

Darren Lake, an overweight, middle-aged executive, felt a strange numbness and tingling in his feet as he navigated freeway traffic on his way to a critical client meeting. Annoyed but increasingly concerned, he recalled the VirtuCare flyer his HR department had given him a week earlier. He dialed into the switchboard, and the operator told him a physician would return his call within the hour.

Doctor Cook had just finished rounds at the clinic in Galveston when his pager notified him of a consult in the VirtuCare queue. He opened his laptop, logged on to the portal, reviewed the medical record, and made the call to Darren Lake.

"Hi Darren, this is Doctor Cook with VirtuCare," Cook announced in his calm, authoritative voice.

"Good morning, Doctor Cook. I have an important meeting today, but woke up not feeling well. My wife and I argued about whether I should go straight to the doctor, but I chose to do my meeting first."

"Okay Darren, glad you called in," Doctor Cook started. "Sounds like you're diving?"

"Yes sir. Like I said, I am headed to an important meeting."

"Noted, Darren. Tell me your symptoms, please, and keep an eye on the road! I think this is our first consult to be done while the patient is driving."

"I love the convenience, and I'm honored to be the first," Darren responded. "I woke up this morning to tingling feet and shortness of breath."

Cook asked a list of questions, then double checked his notes. This was not a primary care issue, but the weight of the situation was clear. Darren Lake needed to go straight to the ER or nearest hospital.

"Mister Lake, I want to be very clear about this. Your symptoms are potentially deadly. You need to go straight to the nearest care facility. If you tell me exactly where you are, I can provide directions and call ahead."

"Are you sure?" Darren thought about his wife Terry's insistence that he cancel the meeting and see a doctor.

"I am utterly serious, Darren. Go now."

By the time Darren arrived at the ER, a doctor was waiting, prepared to confirm the diagnosis. A cardiac stent, inserted less than an hour later, bought Darren Lake twenty more years he wouldn't have otherwise seen. The ER doctor who treated Darren called Doctor Cook later and told him that if he hadn't insisted on Darren going to the ER immediately then he would likely have been dead before the end of the day.

It wasn't a prototypical telemedicine consultation, but it taught the VirtuCare team something important about the value of the service.

A week after the Darren Lake consultation, another memorable call came in. Lila Gaines, a newlywed from Amarillo, who realized with horror upon arriving in San Antonio for her honeymoon that she'd left her birth-control pills at home. Panicked, she called VirtuCare. Dr. Rogers reviewed her Electronic Medical Record and was able to consult with her via telephone. Doctor Rogers called the prescription into a pharmacy just two blocks from the honeymoon suite. Her honeymoon, and peace of mind, were both saved that day.

Marcus, a hardworking warehouse foreman from Fort Worth, woke one day with the unmistakable, painful urgency of a UTI. With zero sick days left and a demanding schedule, taking time off for a doctor's visit was out of the question, so he called VirtuCare during his lunch break. Doctor Bridges triaged the call, arranged for an after-hours urine dip at a partner urgent care clinic, and had a prescription for antibiotics waiting. Marcus made it to work the next morning, uncomfortable, but functional, on the mend, and profoundly grateful.

VirtuCare's call volume doubled, then quadrupled, then doubled again every quarter. The business model was working. Customers were happy and care was almost always delivered in under an hour.

However, with growth came growing pains.

Byron noticed that his tech was slowing down, so he picked up his cell phone and dialed Ray Kurtz, who had returned to his home in Framingham, Massachusetts.

Ray answered on the second ring, "Hey Byron, glad you called."

Byron was going to start talking about some of the growing pains with VirtuCare, but thought he'd better listen first. "Sounds like you have something on your mind?"

"Well, yeah," Kurtz hesitated. "The thing is, I really want to focus on creating AI solutions for providers. I mean, it has been fun starting VirtuCare, but I think maybe we should find my replacement."

Byron sat down, a sinking pit in his stomach. "You're resigning?"

"Not exactly, Byron. I just think it's time for me to phase out. There's a woman I know in Dallas named Michelle Bianchi. I've worked with her before. She's a great architect, and the perfect person to step in."

By now, Byron's head was spinning. The workload had grown to the point where he needed help in almost every category, and didn't need the pain of finding or training a new IT Executive. "What can I do to inspire you to stay on, Ray?"

"Nothing bro. I really am done. I love it, but my life goal is training AI to assist in diagnosis and care. All this routine programming of medical records, patient flow, call centers, billing…well, that's just business stuff. Anyone can do it. Bianchi can do it far better than me."

* * *

Byron Cook thought about the situation as he walked to the liquor cabinet, grabbing his favorite Kentucky bourbon and a glass. His hand trembled a little as he poured, the golden liquid catching the light of the desk lamp.

Papers were stacked around him: business plans, call logs, and resumes. Everyone in his company also held the title of MD.

He took a sip, savoring the liquid heat as it burned its way down his throat. Then, he stared at the phone. "Okay Byron, what now?" he muttered to himself. "You've got a company growing faster than you can manage, a team that thinks Python is a snake, not a programming language, and now your one IT partner is resigning to chase AI and robots." He grinned at the thought.

He took another sip, feeling the familiar, bracing fire. He'd always been careful. Always measured. This, on the other hand…this was chaos.

With a grunt, Cook picked up the phone and dialed. He knew the number by heart.

It rang twice before a familiar, easy voice answered. "Byron Cook, my old friend. To what do I owe the pleasure? You running for President of the Medical Board now? Want to go climb Kilimanjaro again, or maybe Aconcagua?"

Cook almost smiled. "Evening, David. I wish my problems were as simple as training to climb a mountain. You and I have discussed VirtuCare on several occasions, so I think you might guess where this is going…"

David Watson thought about his friend's response. Something serious was going on. "You sound like you've had two glasses already. How can I help?"

"I'm on my first bourbon, so don't get ahead of yourself."

"All right, lay it on me, Byron," David chuckled. "What's up?"

Cook hesitated. The words didn't come easily. "The company's growing, David. But…well, we're all doctors. Nobody knows how to scale a business, let alone run the damn IT. My partner, Ray, just told me he needs to phase out. Wants to chase artificial intelligence, save the world, whatever it is those types do."

There was a pause on the other end. Watson never rushed advice. He could hear Cook tapping and tried to guess whether it was his pen or the glass of bourbon.

"I've been monitoring your progress, and…well, I saw this coming, Byron. Doctors generally don't run companies. They're good at fixing people, not balance sheets." Watson's tone softened. "So, how can I help?"

"I need someone who knows business. Who understands the law and how to build something that lasts. I need a Doctor of Business or Law, David. I need someone I can trust, like my oldest friend."

Watson gave a low whistle. "You must be desperate if you're calling me, Doctor Cook," he joked. "You know how I feel about lawyers, even if I happen to have the diploma."

Cook let out a brittle laugh. "That's what makes you perfect. You know how they think, and you hate them anyway."

There was a long pause. Cook could picture Watson leaning back, considering the ask.

"Let me get this straight," Watson finally said. "You want me to join the circus? Take the helm of a company with a bunch of doctors who know nothing about business, and help fix a brilliantly designed IT system held together with chewing gum and bailing wire?"

"That's about it." Cook paused. "And turn this idea into a billion-dollar company."

Another silence, then Watson's voice, clear and decisive: "I'll do it. But I'll want to come in as CEO. I'll run it my way, engineer's logic, legal backup, no sacred cows. When it comes to operating within the parameter of the healthcare system, your guidance rules, but for everything business, I get to make the call."

Cook breathed out, letting the tension slip away. The two had been friends for decades. They hadn't always seen eye to eye, but who in life had? "That's the deal I was hoping for. We have a huge dream here that could create a lasting impact on access to care."

Watson chuckled. "Get some sleep, Byron. Tomorrow, we can look at how to build this thing and start turning doctors into entrepreneurs."

Cook raised his glass in a silent toast to the phone. "To old friends and new beginnings."

Watson's answer was immediate and warm. "To saving medicine from the doctors," he laughed, knowing that would create a rise in his friend. "Goodnight, Byron."

Cook hung up, feeling the weight shift, just a little. He was a bit pissed at his friend's final comment about saving medicine from doctors, but he could live with it.

For the first time in days, he allowed himself a genuine, cautious smile.

* * *

Klark Thomas had just closed his laptop, a half-finished glass of Scotch sweating on the balcony table at his Miami apartment, when his phone rang. He walked inside, pulled the phone from the receiver, and answered, "Hello?"

"Hi Doctor Thomas. I hope I am not bothering you this evening," the female voice began tenuously.

Klark immediately recognized Jennice's voice. It was one he'd thought about more than he'd admit, even now. Doing his best to sound nonchalant, "Well, if it isn't Nurse, I mean *Doctor* Walters. I was just finishing up a project on my laptop, you're not bothering me at all!"

Jennice's laugh came through warm and bright. "Yes, this is Doctor

Walters, though I must admit it feels weird not having you call me Nurse Walters."

"To what do I owe the pleasure, Doctor?" Klark asked.

"I'm speaking on a CME panel at Jackson Memorial, and have some extra time, so I thought I'd get some advice on a place to get a meal that isn't a crime against cuisine."

He grinned. Her visit couldn't have come at a better time, and for so many years, he'd wondered how life would have been different, better, if he had acted on the clear attraction decades ago. "I'm going to be a bit presumption and invite myself."

Jennice smiled into the phone, "Yes Doctor Thomas, it would be lovely if you could join me."

"Okay, there's a little French bistro on Collins. They serve the best sea bass in the city. Ohhh, and I promise, there's not a single fluorescent light in the restaurant."

"I think I could handle fluorescent, when done right," she laughed lightly. How's 8 PM look for you?"

"It's a date!" Klark answered enthusiastically, then stopped, pulled his foot out of his mouth, "I mean, not a date, unless you want it to be."

Jennice laughed again. "You're cute, Doctor Thomas, but still stumbling over yourself. In any case, after thirty years, I think we've earned a date. See you at 8."

Klark arrived early, requesting a table near the window, nervously straightening his collar. When Jennice walked in, her hair pulled back, her dress a deep blue that matched the Miami twilight, he nearly spilled his water standing up to greet her.

She smiled, eyes lit up as she took him in. "I see you've traded the white coat for business casual. It suits you."

He shook his head, a little bashful. "Just trying to keep up. You still look incredible."

They sat, ordering sea bass for her, a steak for him, and a bottle of Syrah between to share.

"So, Doctor Thomas," Jennice said, swirling her wine, "do you ever miss Boston?"

"Do you mind if we dispense with the Doctor Thomas and Nurse-Doctor Walters formality?" He asked.

She grinned and stuck her hand out "Hi, my name is Jennice Walters."

He took her hand, enjoying the touch. Was it the first? He couldn't remember. "Klark Thomas."

She smiled, eyes sparkling, "It's a pleasure Klark. Do you ever miss Boston?"

Klark smirked. "Only when I want to remember what true suffering feels like. Miami's got traffic, but no tunnels, and you an at least roll the windows down."

She laughed. "Boston had its charms. But I think it was the people that made it worthwhile."

Klark caught her eye, and the old comfort returned. "You know, I've always wondered why you left. You were the best nurse in the city."

She shrugged. "Chasing adventure. Or maybe running from it. Depends on the year."

They drifted into stories about those first jittery days at Mass General, late night deliveries from Regina's Pizza, the chaos of launching the tele-clinic, the first time the equipment failed, and how he had gotten shocked trying to fix a broken TV. Each story brought them closer, with laughter and wine flowing freely.

Jennice set her glass down and regarded him, her tone turning just a shade more serious. "Klark… there's something I always wanted to ask you."

He leaned in, curiosity piqued. "Shoot."

"Back in Boston, when we worked together, well… did you ever think about asking me out? I mean, aside from the time you made me watch the Red Sox at Reginas and then ditched me for a medical conference."

He grinned, cheeks flushing. "You remember that? I was pretty sure you swore off baseball *and* doctors that night."

"Oh, I did. But I never swore off you."

Klark hesitated, then smiled, a little sheepishly. "If I'm honest, Jennice, I thought about it more times than I should admit. At the time, I was chasing goals and a dream. I was an idiot. Oh, and I had this rule to never date at work. Can you imagine how Doctor Charles would have reacted to us dating?"

She nodded, her gaze softening. "I get it. But for the record, I wouldn't have minded breaking the rules. Life's short, Klark. It is definitely too short for looking back and wishing we had taken other paths."

"Do you wish you had taken another path?" he asked.

"Not really." She took a sip of her wine and stared into the glass. "I am happy with my life. I have some beautiful kids, great memories, and they all led me to this restaurant, sitting across from you."

He reached across the table, lightly brushing her hand. "Maybe we get a second, or third, chance?"

Her eyes sparkled. "Maybe we do."

The waiter dropped off the check and a pair of espresso shots. Jennice downed hers in one gulp and grinned mischievously. "So, what are your intentions, Doctor Thomas? Are you going to sweep me off my feet, or are you still afraid of mixing business with pleasure?"

Klark gulped. The attraction was there, but he was not accustomed to her straightforward nature. He stood and offered his arm, a little old-fashioned. "I was thinking… my place is a five-minute walk from here. I have a bottle of whiskey that doesn't deserve to be drunk alone."

She took his arm. "Lead the way."

Klark's apartment was a modern space filled with books and a few faded photos of distant places. He poured two glasses, joining Jennice on the couch. The city lights glowed beyond the windows, music drifting in from the street below.

They started talking, but the conversation softened, words slowing, until Jennice leaned back, her bare feet tucked under her. "You know, for a man who claims to be all about work, you have surprisingly good taste in food, wine, whiskey, and furniture."

Klark grinned. "Don't tell anyone. I have a reputation to protect."

She edged closer, her hand brushing his knee. "What else are you hiding, Klark?"

Klark laughed, setting his glass on the coffee table. "That's my signature style. If I'd known you were coming, I'd have upgraded to *man who sometimes vacuums*."

Jennice patted the cushion beside her. "Don't change a thing. I always liked the chaos."

He picked up his tumbler of whiskey, signaling the glass in a toast. "To chaos and second chances."

They clinked glasses, Jennice's eyes shining. "And to finally breaking the rules. What's the worst that could happen?"

Klark raised an eyebrow, "Well, the last time I broke the rules, I got written up by hospital administration."

She smirked. "I was always better at covering your tracks. Remember that time you totally misplaced your clipboard, knowing that Doctor Charles was about to interrogate you?"

He groaned, grinning. "If memory serves, you were the one who found it, then held it for ransom."

She nudged him playfully. "Only because you promised me coffee for a week. Which, for the record, you never delivered."

He feigned shock. "Is that what tonight's about? Retribution?"

Jennice's laughter was music. "Maybe. Or maybe it's about unfinished business?" Her comment delivered a somewhat uncomfortable beat of silence.

Klark's voice softened. "You know, I kept your first 'television sick note.' The one you wrote for the salesman at Logan. I found it in an old folder last year."

Jennice's eyes widened, her tone turning tender. "You saved it?"

He nodded. "I did. I guess I wanted to remember what it felt like to start something big with someone who believed in me. Some days I felt like Indiana Jones running from that boulder, and others, I felt like I was pushing it up a hill. But with you, well, everything seemed possible."

She leaned in, her smile trembling just a little. "Klark, I always believed in you. Even when you doubted yourself. I saw the future before you did."

He reached for her hand, threading his fingers through hers. "Thirty years. That's a long time to keep something unsaid."

Jennice squeezed his hand, voice catching. "So, say it now."

He met her eyes, no humor now, just raw honesty. "Okay," He took a deep breath and exhaled slowly, "I loved you. Maybe not at first, not when I was still an idiot with tunnel vision, but somewhere between those late shifts and the lopsided coffee deals, I fell. And I kept falling, even after you left Boston. I was just too stubborn, or too scared, to call and tell you." He paused, collecting his thoughts, "Then I heard you got married, so I just buried it."

She touched his face, thumb tracing the lines that hadn't been there all those years ago. "Well, here's the truth, Dr. Thomas, I loved you, too. Still do, apparently. You never really get over your first revolution."

For a moment, neither of them moved. Then, gently, Jennice kissed him. It was sweet and slow, full of all the years they'd lost and the hope of what might be found again.

They pulled back, eyes sparkling, breathless and grinning.

Klark, his voice returning to playful, brushed a stray curl behind her ear. "You know, I should warn you, my idea of romance at this age is a bowl of cereal at midnight and falling asleep during old movies."

Jennice laughed, curling against him. "You're not that old Klark, but that actually sounds perfect. As long as I get the bigger spoon."

He grinned, pulling her close. "Deal. But you're still making coffee in the morning."

"Nope. I can't make even half-decent coffee, and we no longer live in the sixties, sir. Tell you what, I will take a shot at it if you promise not to run off to a medical conference before breakfast."

He pressed his forehead to hers. "If your coffee's really that bad, I cannot make any promises, but tonight, I'm staying right here."

"That's good, because this is your apartment, not mine."

The both laughed, savoring the moment.

Outside, the city was still wide awake, but inside, time slowed. Two revolutionaries, now older, wiser, and maybe a little bruised, finally let themselves be young again. They could feel the years falling away as they laughed, held each other, and let the past finally catch up to the present.

In the hush before midnight, Klark whispered, "Jennice, thank you for calling."

She smiled into his shoulder, content and a little bit in awe. "Klark, it's only taken us thirty years to get here. Let's not waste another minute."

They toasted to love rediscovered, and the delicious adventure of the unknown.

For the first time in years, Klark Thomas let himself believe in new beginnings. And in the quiet glow of the Miami night, two old friends found something they thought they'd lost to time - each other.

4

Taking the Nation by Storm

Entrepreneurs take the helm

Reinvention, One Argument at a Time

The kitchen clock read 6:17 AM, but David Watson's energy could have lit the block. He paced behind Byron Cook's battered kitchen table, the surface barely visible beneath coffee-stained spreadsheets, state medical regulations, and a yellow legal pad on which David had already started diagramming a new company hierarchy.

Byron nursed his second cup of coffee, eyes heavy, face unshaven, a scowl permanently etched from a week of bad news. "You want the truth, David?" he said, "Some days I wish I'd stayed in the damn Air Force."

David, his lifelong friend, flashed a crooked grin. "If you had, you'd be bored senseless by now. This stuff," he gestured to the mountain of chaos, "is the real challenge. And you know it."

Byron scoffed, then grinned. "The challenge right now is finding someone who can actually keep our platform running without melting down every time we get more than a dozen users on the system."

David tapped his pen. "That's why Michelle Bianchi is the first call I made last night. She's flying in from Dallas. You want stability? She's built systems for an internet company, a bank, and a few other entrepreneurial endeavors. I like her."

Byron's skepticism was palpable. "She doesn't mind working with a bunch of doctors? We don't need an IT exec who lasts three months and then quits because she doesn't like *herding stethoscopes*," Cook chuckled. "Doctors are sometimes difficult to work with."

David laughed. "Present company excluded, right? Anyway, she's tougher than she looks. And she's bringing Elaine Singer, a documentation and training expert who understands the impact of the task at hand. I say we trust her to put together her own team."

Byron nodded. "All right. Bring on the A-team. But the docs are already grumbling about the new EMR that Ray tried to install. Half of them threatened to walk out if we made them use it."

David leaned in. "Let's just see what Michelle and Elaine can do before we throw in the towel."

Three hours later, Michelle Bianchi swept into the conference room with the confidence of a woman who'd wrangled bigger egos than this. Barely 5-foot tall, short-cropped hair, pressed slacks, and a navy blazer—she didn't bother with small talk. Elaine Singer, trailing behind, but clearly the business lead, offered a warm, quick smile before setting up her laptop.

David called the meeting to order with the precision of a judge. "Byron, meet Michelle Bianchi, our new IT exec. And this is Elaine Singer, architect, EMR whisperer, and training guru."

Michelle extended a hand, her grip firm. "Pleasure, Dr. Cook. I've already pulled the logs from your current system. It's creative, but needs structure, and of course, buy in from the doctors."

Byron raised an eyebrow. "Is that code for 'disaster?'"

Elaine grinned, pulling up a display of error messages and bug reports. "Not a disaster. Just… how do we put it, Michelle?"

"Let's say it's more like a house built without blueprints. Structurally ambitious, but one stiff gust and it'll fall like a balsa house in the Texas wind."

Byron cut her off, just slightly defensive. "We're doctors, not engineers."

Michelle nodded, turning serious. "And we're not asking you to be. What we need is your input on how to make this system work for you, not the other way around."

That's when the room's temperature dropped. Dr. Rogers, a crusty family physician and unofficial spokesman for the medical staff, folded his arms and spoke for the group: "I've spent fifteen years filling these out," he slapped a thick, printed patient chart on the table. "Now you want us to hunt and peck through screens like we're booking flights to

Cancun? You'll have to pry these *comfortable* charts from the cold, dead hands of most doctors."

Several other doctors laughed and murmured their agreement.

Michelle exchanged a quick glance with Elaine, who jumped in. "What if the computer screen looked exactly like your paper chart?"

The room went quiet. Byron cocked his head. "You can do that?"

Elaine's eyes sparkled, and she clicked a few keys, pulling up a mockup she'd whipped together on the flight down. The screen mirrored the layout of the old patient chart, down to the hand-drawn boxes and flow-sheet margins.

Dr. Kendall leaned forward, peering at the display. "Huh. That's… that's the same order I use now."

Michelle slid a tablet across the table. "Try it. You tap instead of writing. It auto-populates the patient data, flags your allergies, and you can still scribble, dictate, or type notes if you want."

A reluctant silence settled as Dr. Rogers tapped and swiped. After a moment, he grumbled, "Well, I'll be damned."

Michelle smiled, warm but unyielding. "Doctors should focus on care, not coding. We'll build the system around you, not the other way around. You can expect us to spend time with you asking what you want, rather than handing you what we think you need, or want."

Byron, seeing his staff's guard drop just, exhaled for the first time all day. "All right. If you can get Dr. Rogers to use this thing, you might just accelerate the dream of this company."

Elaine turned to David, who was scribbling furiously on his legal pad. "We'll have a pilot ready in a week. If it passes muster with the doctors, we'll roll it out company wide."

David grinned, pushing his reading glasses up his nose. "Perfect. That leaves us the other mountain to climb."

"What's that?" Michelle asked.

"As we roll out to the 50 states, we are going to need physicians licensed in every state where consultations happen," Watson explained. "If you imagine a state like Idaho, where we have a dozen patients, it will be difficult to inspire a doctor to join when they might get a consult or two a year. On top of that, we need to have a guarantee of an hour response time, or the doctor visit is free."

Elaine looked up. "I am already on it. I have created what I call the 'Super Doc' program. We do the work to get our best doctors licensed in multiple states. Doctors will become multi-state licensed, and we will have our fastest and best working around the country. That, after all, is exactly the value of the phone, and internet access to a secure medical record."

"Brilliant," Cook grinned, recognizing that brining in creative business experts alongside his great physicians was going to transform the company in ways he had not even imagined.

Elaine nodded. "I've mapped the fastest pathway through state boards and drafted a system to manage all the paperwork. White-glove service for the doctors, concierge, everything. We'll even handle the continuing ed credits."

Byron, a cautious optimism lighting his eyes, nodded slowly. "If you can really make that happen, you'll make history."

David smiled at the team. "That's the plan. Now, let's get to work. Because the only way out is through."

As the meeting broke, Byron watched Michelle and Elaine bent over their laptops, already iterating on the interface. For the first time in months, he was absolutely certain that the company was in good hands.

* * *

The days blurred together in a flurry of updates and onboarding. Byron Cook was not absolutely confident the company would survive its growing pains. That is, until the next crisis landed with the subtlety of a bomb.

It started with a phone call at 10:32 PM. Cook was sifting through licensure paperwork when his personal line rang. He frowned. No one called this number at night unless it was an emergency.

"Byron Cook."

A tense voice came through the line. "Byron, it's Dr. Rogers. We've got a problem."

Cook sat upright. "What is it?"

Rogers sounded shaken. "I just got off a consult with a patient who was pretty insistent, actually, the patient became aggressive."

"About what, Doctor Rogers?"

"The patient wanted a script for oxycodone. Said her 'usual doctor' always gave it to her, but something felt off. I checked her chart. She has called three times this week, saw three different docs. Same story every time. Nothing has been written yet, but this could be a problem."

Cook's jaw tightened. "Dammit. That's the last thing we need. Did you document everything?"

Rogers sighed. "Of course. But Byron, if one passionate patient succeeds and there's an audit, we are gonna have problems."

"Yeah, I know," Cook cut him off. "I'll handle it. Thanks, Kimball."

He hung up and pressed his palms to his eyes, fighting off a headache. If they didn't get ahead of this, all their progress could come crashing down. This wasn't just a business risk. It was potentially a federal issue, the kind that could destroy careers, end medical licenses, and maybe even wind up with prison sentences.

The next morning, Cook stormed into David Watson's office, the door rattling on its hinges.

David barely looked up. "You look like you slept in your clothes."

"I did. We've got a narcotics problem. Some of our doctors are getting manipulated by drug seekers. They are requesting scripts for oxy and hydrocodone. I think addicts are going think of us as the resource for their Halloween candy. One of our new hires almost filled a request this week. This is a disaster, David."

David's brow furrowed. "I'll call the attorneys. We need a compliance firewall. What's your fix?"

Cook grumbled, "I'm thinking it would be a mistake to just create a new policy. Doctors are caregivers. They want to help…"

David thought about it for a minute. "You know, we are trying to make the process more efficient. If a doctor decides to write a script for an antibiotic, they then spend time calling the pharmacy."

"That's correct David, but I'm not following the significance here."

"It's not a good use of the doctors time, calling a pharmacy, and it lacks oversight," David picked up his pen and made a note. "Why don't we assign nurses the task of finalizing the medical record when the physician finishes the consult, and then have the nurse call the pharmacy."

"That's brilliant," Cook said, his tone turning more decisive. "Nurses will not be on with the patient, so they're not going to be sweet-talked or bullied. From now on, every encounter gets reviewed by a nurse before any prescription goes out. No exceptions."

David nodded slowly. "I will call Elaine and have her add this. Nurses review the consultation, double-check the patient's history, and only if everything checks out do they call the pharmacy. If they have doubts, they escalate to Doctor Rogers."

Byron grinned. "Old-fashioned oversight. I like it."

Later that afternoon, David Watson gathered Michelle, Elaine, and a handful of senior physicians in the main conference room.

"I know none of you want more bureaucracy, but we're one DEA investigation away from disaster. From now on, no doctor writes a prescription directly. This will become a huge time saver for the physician and an essential firewall for the company. Every encounter that results in a prescription gets reviewed by a nurse. The nurse will call in any approved script, and the EMR will log every step."

Doctor Burke slammed his palm on the table. "So now I need a babysitter to write a prescription?"

Cook met his glare head-on. "If that's what it takes to protect this company and your license, yes. If you don't like it, you know where the door is."

Michelle cleared her throat, breaking the silence. "We'll update the software and flag all consults that have requests for prescriptions and also create an audit trail."

Elaine added, "I'll work on getting some nurses hired. We'll draft protocols and train them. Give us a week."

Burke shook his head, but didn't argue further. Most of the doctors seemed happy about the new procedure,

Doctor Bruce stood up, "Uhhh, will we still be paid the same amount per consult?"

"Yes," Watson answered.

"I'm definitely cool with this," Bruce looked at the other doctors in the room, then fixed his gaze on Burke. "Look, this is better for us, Burke. Makes us more efficient *and* protects the company."

Burke nodded, and no one walked out.

When the meeting broke, Cook lingered with Michelle and Elaine. "Thanks. This may seem unpopular, but it's absolutely necessary and will be huge to protect VirtuCare."

Michelle smiled wryly. "If popular was what you wanted, you should've gone into politics."

Cook almost smiled. "No, thanks. One circus is enough."

As the others filtered out, Cook sat in the now-empty conference room, looking at the wall of state licenses Elaine had helped them secure. This was one of those moments when he realized the potential impact of what they were doing. The company had done nearly twenty thousand consultations with an average response time of 14 minutes and a satisfaction rating of 97%. No one in healthcare was anywhere close to those numbers.

* * *

A month after the "Super Doc" program launched, and the nurse-prescription system was humming along, David Watson sat in his office late one night, studying a revenue forecast with equal parts satisfaction and dread. The business was growing, but the outside world barely knew they existed. This company had the potential to change everything, but if they were going to dominate, someone needed to make noise.

David quickly buzzed Byron's phone, he answered on the first ring. "I need to hire a marketing guy."

"No." Byron said flatly. "The Federal Board hates marketing in healthcare. It will shine a light on us that we don't want or need."

"We are at a crossroads, Byron. We both want to build a real company, and to do that, we need marketing and PR."

"Shit," Doctor Cook took a deep breath and exhaled slowly from the other end of the line.

 "Yup." David paused, knowing it would give his old friend time to think and not react with anger. "I have checked my network and found Greg Wallace. The guy is a genius at marketing and sales, but he's… well, you'll see."

* * *

Greg Wallace's arrival was more thunderclap than gentle onboarding. He appeared at 8:03 AM sharp, a tall, articulate man in an impeccably tailored suit, and within an hour had commandeered the large conference room. His presentation left the company's original team in stunned silence.

"We're sitting on a gold mine," Greg said, voice brisk and emotionless. "But no one's ever heard of us. You're telling a revolutionary story to an empty room. First, we need national PR, then we shift to verticals, discount brokers, large employers, health systems, and payers. We absolutely must get out in front or we die as a rounding error in some investor's spreadsheet."

Elaine raised a hand, tentative. "Greg, we're already stretched with minimal tech support, and physician recruitment has been difficult."

Greg interrupted, never glancing her way. "You're thinking small. We need a team that wakes up every morning and thinks about headlines, not help desk tickets. That's what I'm here to build."

His plan was brilliant. Within days, Greg had hired a national PR firm called CPR, a group that had been responsible for issuing in several innovations to the press and was clearly recognized as one of the best. Greg began intensely planning a strategy with CPR, and it was so thorough that the founding executives at the PR firm became engaged.

Behind the scenes, tempers were fraying. Greg was ruthless, impatient. He critiqued every draft, dismissed "excuses," and his feedback was always delivered in clipped, icy tones.

"I don't have time to sugarcoat this," he snapped at a junior marketing associate. "If you can't see why that strategy's wrong, you're in the wrong business."

He rewrote copy on the fly, tore up campaign ideas, and demanded late-night meetings. Michelle Bianchi almost threw a whiteboard marker at him during one session, and Byron stopped attending marketing meetings altogether.

David tried to intervene. "Greg, you need to bring people with you, not run over them. This company has a strong foundation of corporate culture with collaboration and, well, inspiration."

Greg was unmoved. "You hired me to make noise. I don't have time for handholding."

"Look Greg, I will acquiesce to your strategic brilliance, but you're gonna have to recognize our culture of mutual respect."

Greg nodded, straightening his perfect tie. "All right, David. I can do that." He smiled and walked out of the office.

In spite of that promise, it didn't take long for the friction to start.

One afternoon Elaine Singer was hunched over a laptop in the war room, finalizing a pitch for a hospital chain. Greg swept in, barely glancing at her. "Let me see the deck."

She slid the laptop over, voice hopeful. "I think this angle with the human stories will resonate with the CEO of this company. They care about outcomes, but they want to see the faces behind the tech."

Greg's eyes flicked down the slides. "Stories don't sell. Numbers do." He began editing, cutting out patient testimonials, adding a chart of projected cost savings. "This is why we're losing ground. If you want a job in fiction try publishing, or go back to college and study to be an author."

Elaine's face went red. "Greg, these stories are the reason we have doctors on our platform. This isn't insurance sales, it's about people who appreciate the access to the care that we are providing."

He didn't look up. "Then you run your campaigns, and I'll run mine. Let's see who delivers revenue."

Elaine stood up, lips pressed in a thin line. She wasn't about to let Greg trigger her. "Maybe you should actually talk to a doctor before you kill everything that makes us different."

Greg only shrugged. "If it moves the needle, I'll do it."

The next day, Michelle Bianchi was demoing the newly redesigned EMR interface for the marketing team. She was proud of the result. The screens mimicked the paper charts but added automation that no chart could provide, and the doctors were finally coming around.

Greg watched for three minutes, then interrupted. "This is what you're showing the press? It's ugly."

Michelle bristled. "It's not for the press. We designed this specifically for our physicians. They want familiar, not flashy. This is what's working and the doctors are happy."

Greg waved a dismissive hand. "You're missing the point. Every piece of software that changed the world looked amazing. Do you think Apple sold iPods because they felt like a CD player? If we want press, and THAT is what I was hired to get us, we need to make it beautiful."

Michelle stared, incredulously. "You want me to rebuild the whole interface because you think CNBC cares what the allergy box looks like?"

Greg leaned forward, voice icy. "Yes, if you want people to care. Or we'll just keep being doctors with a website no one's heard of."

"Screw you, Wallace." Michelle closed her laptop with a snap and walked out.

The tension boiled over in the Friday meeting. Greg had just shredded another campaign draft, calling it "the work of amateurs," and the sales VP had stormed out, muttering that she wasn't rebuilding the campaign for an asshole who didn't understand human decency.

"Well, screw her," was all that Greg said as she walked out.

Elaine, who had finally had enough, got up without saying a word and left, slamming the door hard enough to rattle the glass.

David found Elaine pacing in the break room, tears threatening. "I can't work with him, David. He's impossible. He doesn't listen. He cares more about being right than about the company. He doesn't fit here and you're about to have a major walk-out if you don't fix it."

Michelle, sipping coffee, shot a glare over the rim of her mug. "If I wanted to be insulted every day, I'd go back to hospital IT."

David nodded, shoulders heavy. "I know. I've been watching. Greg delivers results, but I didn't bring him in to drive away the people who built this company. Let me talk to him."

David found Greg in the conference room, hunched over analytics. "You've alienated my best people, Greg. I appreciate the results you're getting, but this can't go on."

Greg looked up, unapologetic. "They're too soft, David. You want to win? You need to move faster. You brought me in for a reason."

David exhaled. "I brought you in for your mind and your creativity. I have bult a team that trusts and respects each other, not one that dreads coming to work. Find some patience, or we'll have a different conversation."

Greg sat back, expression unreadable. "I get it. I'll try to tone it down."

But nothing changed.

Two weeks later, after another shouting match left the team shaken, David called Greg into his office.

"Greg, your work has been invaluable," David began. "You've changed our trajectory, but you're not a fit for the culture we're building here at VirtuCare."

Greg nodded, surprisingly calm. "I figured. My style is not for everyone, and I've never been much for coddling my colleagues."

David extended his hand. "I'm sure you know this means it's time for us to part ways."

"Yup."

David rubbed his chin and stood. "If you're okay with it, I'd like to keep you as a consultant. We need your ideas. But this team needs to heal."

Greg gathered his things and headed for the door, pausing only to say, "Call me anytime. I'll always tell you the truth, even if it hurts."

David smiled. "I wouldn't expect anything less."

As Greg left the building, David watched the team start to relax in a collective sigh of relief. Almost instantly, he saw laughter returning, and the company found its balance again. He knew this team would be stronger for the storm. He recognized the value brought by Greg but felt it would be better delivered from a safer distance.

* * *

With the departure of Greg Wallace, David decided the next thing he needed to do was terminate the contract with CPR, the national PR firm Wallace had hired. David Watson tossed the thick CPR PR contract onto his desk, staring at the dense legal print. There was not a loophole or termination clause that would allow VirtuCare to end the relationship.

Their name was Crescent Public Relations, but everyone called them CPR. David felt the name was somewhat ironic. He could almost hear Greg Wallace's ghost muttering, *"Big firms tend to be expensive, but if you get the right one that knows how to do its job, it's like magic."*

Now, with Greg gone and the dust just beginning to settle, David wondered if he could personally handle CPR. He didn't need salt on the now healing wound of employee morale with the hiring of a new marketing guru.

He thumbed through the paperwork, checking a second time for the termination clause he desperately needed. Instead, he found a simple, impenetrable paragraph: *Client is obligated to a twelve-month retainer, non-cancellable except for cause as defined in section 13B.*

David groaned. "Stuck. A whole damn year." He poured a cup of coffee and shook off the frustration. Quitting wasn't in his DNA. If he was tied to CPR, he'd find a way to squeeze every drop of value from it.

He called CPR's CEO, a brisk, self-assured woman named Lori Case.

Lori answered on the second ring. "VirtuCare! Mr. Watson, I trust you've reviewed our rollout?"

David took a deep breath, stating in his best CEO tone. "Lori, let's get moving. Full national campaign. No holding back. I want VirtuCare on every editor's desk and every health reporter's speed dial. Sell the future. Sell access. Sell us."

Lori's reply was confident: "We're ready, David. I'll have my team in Houston on Monday. We'll start with an industry announcement, then hit mainstream press, digital, and local outlets. You'll be everywhere. I promise."

March 2005, CPR's Houston Office

The conference room buzzed with energy as Lori's team worked up the first major release. The angle: *"VirtuCare: The Doctor Will See You Anytime, Anywhere."* They staged interviews with Byron, Michelle, and Elaine, posed photographs of doctors consulting on laptops, and lined up calls with skeptical hospital CEOs.

David sat in for the first media prep, listening as Lori rehearsed him for tough questions.

"What do you say, Mr. Watson, to critics who claim telemedicine isn't real medicine?" she pressed.

David answered, steady, "Access to care is the single biggest health problem in America. Technology closes that gap, safely and legally. We're regulated, we're credentialed, we have the highest satisfaction rating of any company in healthcare, we are delivering doctors to patients in under fifteen minutes for $35, and we're saving lives."

Lori nodded, satisfied. "Stick to that, and you'll be fine."

Within weeks, the story hit. *USA Today, The Wall Street Journal, CNN, Forbes*, even local TV stations in states across the country. At first, the office celebrated every mention, with Elaine taping articles to the break room wall, Michelle forwarding links to the engineering group, and Byron grumbling about the press spelling his name wrong.

But as the campaign gained momentum, the questions became more prevalent:

Is VirtuCare a threat to patient safety?

Will telemedicine erode the doctor-patient relationship?

Can a Texas doctor really treat a patient in Maine?

Is VirtuCare skirting the law?

More than half the articles cast doubt, painting VirtuCare as either a revolution or a risk.

In a meeting, Lori breezed in, smiling. "David, we're at seven hundred mainstream articles. Syndication is through the roof. Coverage is polarized, but everyone's talking. You're trending in the top three for 'health innovation' on *Google News*. You and VirtuCare have visited the walls of practically every home and place of business in America."

Byron shook his head. "Half of them think we're snake oil salesmen."

Elaine grinned. "And the other half are calling to ask how they can get a virtual appointment for their mother-in-law."

Michelle was the first to say it out loud. "Whatever they write, they can't ignore us anymore."

David leaned back, feeling the strange exhilaration of controversy and momentum. "That's how change happens. At least now, the world knows our name."

By January, VirtuCare's patient numbers had quadrupled, then tripled again. Call volume spiked, and new doctors applied daily.

He smiled, knowing the company was finally at the center of a conversation America could no longer avoid. He raised his coffee mug to the wall and whispered, "Here's to twelve months well spent."

David Watson was not prepared for, and had no idea the impact, of what was about to happen next.

5

Our Friends at the Federal Board

2005 – The Summons

The official letter was delivered by hand via service of process on a hot and humid Monday morning. It came in an oversized envelope embossed with the insignia of the Federal Board of Medical Examiners. David Watson broke the seal with steady hands, but the moment he read the summons, his pulse ticked up.

Byron Cook had been notified of the delivery, and walked down the hall to David's office. He walked around the desk, standing at David's shoulder, and caught the words *"mandatory appearance"* and *"Federal Board."*

David read aloud: "Mr. Watson, Dr. Cook, you are hereby ordered to appear before the Federal Board of Medical Examiners on August 15, 2005, to answer for alleged violations of interstate medical practice statutes and unauthorized practice of medicine."

Byron's face went white. "They're going to crucify us."

David didn't answer right away. He just folded the letter, set it neatly on the table, and met Byron's frightened gaze. "No, my friend. Like all challenges in life and business, we will find a solution. Let's look at this like an opportunity to tell the Board about our accomplishments."

"The Board only calls doctors in who they intend to sanction," Byron responded, sensing the impending gloom.

"And we will turn the tables, my friend," David patted his friend's back.

"Whatever you say. We need to hire the best lawyers," Byron answered while trying to calm his pounding heart.

"No lawyers. I think they would enflame the situation. Let's go solo and see if we can reason with them?"

"Solo? Not gonna happen, David. When the Board summons, bad things always happen. We need to bring in defense."

"Bad things *always* happen?" David emphasized.

"Yes."

"And, do doctors always bring lawyers to the hearings?"

"Yes."

"See where I'm going with this, Byron?"

"Not exactly."

"Lawyers are what you bring to battle. Let's not go to the hearing looking like we are in a battle. We need to create advocacy, make friends, and find the middle ground."

Washington, D.C. – Two Weeks Later

The hearing room at the Board's headquarters was everything David expected: dark wood, glaring fluorescent lights, and a committee table raised high above the witness chairs. Cameras. Microphones. The seal of the Board presided over it all, newly polished and intended to be twice as menacing.

Benedict Crane sat at the center, his silver hair gleaming, a cold smile playing at the corner of his mouth. He didn't bother to stand as David and Byron were escorted to their seats.

Crane's voice was all steel. "Gentlemen. Welcome. Please state your names for the record."

David spoke first, voice measured. "David Watson. CEO, VirtuCare."

Byron hesitated, swallowing hard. "Byron Cook. Co-founder and Medical Director."

Crane rifled through a folder—thick with printed news clippings, patient logs, and legal memos. "Mr. Watson and Dr. Cook. Are you waiving your right to legal counsel?"

"No sir," David started. "We feel like what we are doing is appropriate and beneficial for the future of healthcare. And most of all, we feel like what we are doing *is* legal. We are not here to fight, but instead to collaborate."

David watched as several of the Board members smiled or nodded.

Crane scoffed and frowned. "You are here today because VirtuCare is, by every reasonable interpretation of current law, engaged in the unlicensed practice of medicine across state lines. You employ doctors who have never so much as shaken hands with their patients. You call it innovation. I call it dangerous."

David kept his face impassive. "We truly believe what we're doing is both necessary *and* legal. We follow state licensure; we document every encounter…"

Crane cut him off, eyes narrowing. "Do not lecture me about documentation. Let's be clear, the Board has the authority to issue immediate cease and desist orders. We can refer criminal charges to the Department of Justice. And I am strongly considering both."

A heavy silence settled. Byron gripped the table edge, knuckles white.

Crane leaned forward, voice dropping to a whisper only just picked up by the microphones. "There are lines, gentlemen, that medicine should never cross. A real doctor touches his patient. He listens, he observes. You replace this with a screen, or worse, a cold phone call, and you cheapen the time tested and loved practice of medicine."

Byron finally found his voice, low and tremulous. "People are getting care, Mr. Crane. Lives are being saved. We are helping people who'd never see a doctor otherwise."

Crane's gaze flicked to Byron with cold amusement. "And if one of your virtual patients dies from a missed diagnosis? If a child is misprescribed? Who do I hold responsible? The machine? The call center nurse?"

David broke in, his voice firm and confident. "We own our results, sir. We document, we audit, and we've saved more lives than we've put at risk. We have the highest satisfaction rating of anything in healthcare, and with tens of thousands of consultations, not a single malpractice filing. The data speaks for itself."

Crane straightened, closing the folder. "Your data is a pile of bullshit, sir. You have two weeks to prepare a full response on a legal, clinical, and ethical front. If this committee is not convinced, VirtuCare will be shut down. And you both," he pointed a finger at Watson, then Cook, "will face criminal charges. Is that clear?"

David nodded once, and with a smile that was cool as steel, responded, "Crystal."

Crane's smile was icy. "Then we are adjourned. I'll see you in two weeks, and next time, I suggest you bring lawyers."

When the two friends exited the building, the D.C. air was crisp and clear, but it did little to remove the heavy feeling. Byron fumbled with his briefcase, hands trembling. "David, they'll bury us. That man has a personal vendetta and hates what we're doing. He wants to make an example out of us."

David stood very still, staring up at the imposing building. "Maybe he does. But the law is written by men, Byron, not gods. We have two weeks. We're going to find a way through this."

Byron's voice was almost a whisper. "I've spent my whole life building this. What if it's all gone? What if I lose my license? What if we go to prison?"

David put a hand on Byron's shoulder, steady. "You won't. I won't let it happen. We're going to fight. And we're going to find a way to win. Call your friend Klark Thomas and see if he has any suggestions or insight."

"Okay." Byron choked out as he and his lifelong friend, and business partner, stood together in the shadow of the Board, uncertain but unbroken. The full weight of the future pressing down on their shoulders.

* * *

Once back at VirtuCare HQ David Watson leaned back in his chair, the printed letter from the Federal Board of Medical Examiners still vibrating in his hand like it carried an electrical charge. The formal language and clear threats from Crane echoed in his head:

"Crossing state lines to provide care… treating patients whom the physician has not physically examined… subject to criminal referral."

Across the room, Byron Cook stood at the window, arms folded, jaw set in stone. "They're coming for us, David. Full force. And they're not bluffing."

"Did you talk to Doctor Thomas?"

"Yes," Byron answered, closing his eyes and taking a deep breath. "He has crossed paths with Crane. The man has long since been adamant against telemedicine."

David didn't respond immediately. Instead, he watched his old friend's reflection in the glass—a man who had built the scaffolding of VirtuCare with mathematical precision, now visibly shaking beneath the weight of uncertainty.

"They're scared," David finally said referring to the Board.

"No," Byron replied, turning sharply. "They're *angry*. There's a difference. Fear might mean progress is possible. Anger means they want blood. Crane wants our blood. Like I told you, he wants to make an example out of us."

David exhaled and motioned to the leather chair across from his desk. "Sit down, Byron."

"I'm not in the mood for a pep talk."

"This isn't a pep talk," David said. "It's a war strategy session."

Byron hesitated, then lowered himself into the chair like it was made of spikes.

"You remember what we said when we started this thing?" David began. "That health care was broken. Not just inefficient, its *broken*. People waiting weeks to see a doctor. Parents dragging sick kids to an ER at midnight. Seniors dying alone in rural towns because the nearest clinic was 200 miles away."

Byron said nothing. His eyes were fixed on the floor.

"And we fixed that for thousands of people," David continued. "We gave a man with chest pain a solution that will give him another twenty years with his family. We saved an airplane full of passengers the possibility of getting sick when a mother was planning to bring her contagious daughter with measles on a flight. We're *working*, Byron."

Byron looked up. His voice was quiet, measured. "But if the government shuts us down, all that progress dies with us. I'm not afraid for me, David. I'm afraid we built this too early. We are the pioneers and now we will be getting shot with arrows."

David leaned forward, his voice lowering. "You think Edison didn't get sued? You think Galileo didn't face backlash? Hell, Byron, I went to law school *because* I hate lawyers, and now I'm going to have to argue against an entire federal board that's being run by a man who thinks remote care is a criminal offense."

Byron smirked faintly at that.

"But this isn't your battle," David said. "You're the architect. You're the one who made this system safe, clean, and reliable. That's your role. *This* legal knife fight, this political death match? This fight is mine."

"And if they come after you personally?" Byron asked, voice tight.

"Then they better pack a lunch."

Byron finally cracked a grin. "You always were the guy who'd run through a wall if you thought it needed fixing."

"And you're the guy who'd calculate the load-bearing stress of that wall before I hit it," David replied.

A silence stretched between them. The tension hadn't vanished, but the temperature in the room had dropped a few degrees.

"I'll need the entire two weeks," Byron finally admitted. "To process all of this. I need to make sure I can withstand this, and our systems can run in a worst-case scenario."

"I know," David said. "Take it. And while you're doing that, I will begin to focus on our team and the culture we're gonna need to withstand this onslaught."

"Onslaught is about right, David."

"Hah," David chuckled. "If we're going to survive this, we need more than strategy. We need alignment. Every employee in this company, including the doctors, nurses, and even our admin, Ruthie, must understand the implications and believe in what we're doing. If there's the slightest whisper of doubt inside this company, Crane will use it to tear us apart."

Byron nodded. "You planning to lead that effort?"

"I need you to help me *define* it. I will create a cultural firewall as strong as the tech we've built. Let's get people talking about how to reinforce the mission, and remind them who we are and what we stand for."

"And who we're not," Byron added.

"Exactly," David said, standing and pointing at his friend. "We're not snake oil salesmen. We're not a call center pretending to be a clinic. We're not here to replace doctors. We're here to *empower* them—to expand their reach, and to heal people wherever they are."

The two men stood in silence, the moment solidifying into something unspoken and foundational.

Then David added, softly, "This isn't the end, Byron. It's just Thermopylae. And I'll be damned if we don't hold the pass."

Byron stared at him a moment longer, then gave a slow, resolute nod. "Geez, David. That was a slaughter of 300 against a million."

"Yup."

"That was bronze age, right?" Byron asked.

"480 BC was bronze. I think the Romans were the first to use iron."

"Alright," Byron said. "Let's sharpen the bronze swords."

David spent the next few days thinking about the exact presentation he needed to do with the employees.

More than sixty employees gathered: doctors, nurses, software engineers, patient advocates, and a handful of interns who had never seen their CEO without a smile.

But today, David Watson wasn't smiling.

He stood at the front of the room, sleeves rolled, jaw tight, remote clicker in hand.

On the screen behind him: a photo of a rural clinic, the kind with faded linoleum floors and a paper sign taped to the door, alongside a sign that said:

Next available appointment: 17 days

The next slide held an image cut to a graph from old CMS data:

Average Wait Time to See a Primary Care Physician: 14.7 days

The next slide showed patient satisfaction numbers from 1999. Red bars. Frowns. Words like "frustrating," "confusing," and "disconnected." The best rating was 68% satisfaction.

David turned to face the group. "This was healthcare before VirtuCare. You guys are changing the world."

He paused. Let it breathe.

"When Byron and I decided to work together on this company, people told us it was impossible. They told us care couldn't happen over a phone or a screen. They said remote diagnosis was 'voodoo medicine.' They said real doctors needed to be in the room. That *we* weren't real."

He took a slow step forward.

"But let me tell you something. That little girl with the measles who didn't board a plane and infect 200 people? That was real. That warehouse foreman in Fort Worth who didn't lose a week of work to a UTI? That was real. And Darren Lake, the man who walked into an ER with a stent-saving diagnosis because one of *you* answered the phone? *That* was real medicine."

A few nods. Quiet murmurs. The energy in the room was beginning to turn.

David clicked to the next slide showing a new graph. This one showed post-VirtuCare satisfaction scores. 89%. Then 91%. Then 94%.

"I'm not here to tell you this fight will be easy. The Federal Board of Medical Examiners wants to shut us down. They're afraid. Because when systems like ours work, they reveal how broken the old ways really were. The rules and regs create power and when we threaten someone's power, their status quo, well, we become their enemy."

David locked eyes with the front row.

"They will come at us. They will use legal threats, licensing technicalities, and concocted public skepticism. I can't promise you that we will get through this without scars. One thing I can tell you though is that we, all of us, are changing the world. We are improving access and making healthcare better. That is something worth fighting for."

He stepped back and pulled up a final slide.

It wasn't a chart, it was a photo—300 actors from a school play, dressed as Spartans, shields raised, spears pointed forward.

"I read a story last night," he said. "Leonidas picked 300 men, not because they were the best fighters, but because each one had a wife and a living son or daughter. These were men who understood legacy. They understood what they were fighting for and the implications if they lost. Leonidas knew he didn't need an army. He needed a *phalanx*."

He looked around the room—dozens of men and women in scrubs and sneakers, dress shirts and hoodies, all watching him now with wide eyes.

"This company is our phalanx. And I don't need everyone here to stay. I only need the ones who believe. The ones who wake up and *know* that what we're doing matters."

A long silence.

"I'll take the heat. I'll stand in front of Congress if I have to. But I can't fight this war alone. If you stay, make a commitment to *really* stay. That commitment should be because you love what we're doing, and you believe that a parent shouldn't have to choose between missing work and getting their kid seen by a doctor, in under 15 minutes, for a mere $35."

He exhaled. Quiet now.

"If we stay together, we don't fail. We hold the line. And that, my friends, is how revolutions prevail."

The room erupted—not in cheers, but in a rising murmur of unity. Heads nodded. Shoulders squared. People turned to one another with that wordless look of *I'm in. We are the phalanx.*

Byron, standing at the back of the room now, arms crossed, nodded once and gave a quiet smile. He wasn't standing solo on the cliff anymore.

He had found his team, a perfect phalanx.

David Watson didn't sleep that night. He sat cross-legged on the hardwood floor of his study, surrounded by legal journals, medical protocols, and transcripts from old licensing hearings. His laptop screen glowed in the dark, casting deep shadows across coffee mugs and notepads. Once upon a time he had gone to law school with big eyes and high hopes. For the most part, those four grueling years had made him dislike lawyers and the law. It was times like this when the entire investment in time and dollars paid off—not just for David Watson, but for healthcare.

He'd been combing through telemedicine policy precedents, searching for a crack in the armor of the Federal Board's argument. And just before dawn, he found it. A phrase in a 1994 decision from the Texas Medical Board: *"Cross-coverage, in which a licensed physician provides temporary care for a patient of another physician, need not require a prior in-person examination if clinically appropriate."*

David froze.

He read it again. And again.

Then, the lightning bolt hit.

Physicians across America, every day, in every practice, clinic, and hospital were treating patients they'd never seen before. It was called *cross-coverage*. Physicians couldn't work 24/7, so they asked colleagues to cover for them. A covering doctor, often on call, sometimes hundreds of miles away, would receive a call, pull up a chart if it was available, speak to a nurse or patient by phone, and prescribe medication or make a clinical judgment. The covering physician had no way of even *knowing* that the person on the phone was who they claimed to be, or that they really were a patient of the covered doctor.

No physical exam. No prior relationship. No criminal referral. No hearing.

Just care.

Cross-coverage. It had been around since the beginning of the telephone.

David grabbed his phone and called Byron. It was 4:13 AM.

"You awake?"

"I wasn't, but I am now," Byron grunted.

"I found the crack in the wall. Cross-coverage."

"What?"

"Cross-coverage, Byron. It's a standard protocol. Accepted by every licensing board. Doctors cover for each other all the time, by phone, remotely. They don't know the patients. No in-person exam. It's the same thing we're doing, except we *do* know our patients. We have their full EMR, we document everything, and our patients opt-in. Our doctors have med mal and get paid for the encounter."

A beat of silence.

"I know what cross-coverage is, David. That actually makes a hell of a lot of sense," Byron said slowly. "We're not inventing something radical. We're just formalizing what's already being done informally."

David grinned into the darkness. "Better than that, Byron. We are improving cross-coverage for the doctor *and* for the patient. And now, we're going to show them."

One Week Later

Federal Board of Medical Examiners – Special Hearing Room 4A

Special Hearing Room 4A was mahogany-paneled, likely designed to put fear in the hearts of doctors. Between all of the mainstream articles on VirtuCare and the Cook-Watson company personalities word had gotten out, and reporters lined the back wall of the room. A handful of patient advocates filled the gallery, along with doctors, regulators, and curious observers who had heard about the escalating case between VirtuCare and the Board.

David sat at a small rectangular table with a slim binder and no lawyer.

Across from him sat the Board.

At the center: Benedict Crane, director, stone-faced, and calculating his opponent to this new form of medicine.

Crane's voice boomed. "Mr. Watson, the record shows your company has treated more than 30,000 patients across multiple state lines without an in-person physician examination. Do you consider this acceptable medical practice?"

David opened the binder. "I actually consider it *standard* medical practice."

Crane raised an eyebrow. "Standard? And how do you, a non-doctor, come to that brilliant conclusion?" he asked sarcastically.

David clicked the remote.

Slide one: A scanned policy from the American College of Physicians.

"Cross-coverage is a standard component of physician practice, allowing care to be provided by a physician other than the one with an established relationship, when appropriately documented and communicated."

Slide two: An image of a hospital paging system, and a transcript from a typical cross-coverage call.

"Dr. Patel, this is Nurse Harmon. I'm calling about Mr. Jenkins in 408. He's short of breath again."

"I see the old chart. Let's get a chest X-ray."

David turned to the Board.

"None of these doctors ever met the patient in person. No one filed charges. No one called it 'unauthorized practice.' But when *we* do it," he emphasized the word *we*, "more carefully, more thoroughly, and responding nationwide in under 15 minutes, *with* the full medical record, *and* the doctor getting paid, it's suddenly criminal?"

A murmur stirred in the room.

Crane straightened. "Mr. Watson, you are attempting to justify a violation of federal law through a loophole?"

David stepped forward. "It's not a loophole, Director Crane. It's the standard you already approve. The only difference is we've built structure around it. *We* have improved it. We have documentation,

EMR, audit logs, triage protocol, and full consent. And guess what? Our patients are happier, healthier, and getting seen *within the hour, 24-hours a day.*"

He clicked the final slide: a testimonial video.

A mother with a toddler on her lap spoke into the camera. "Without VirtuCare, I would've waited six hours in the ER. Instead, I got help at home. My daughter had a highly infectious flu. The VirtuCare doctors caught it early. We were safe. My daughter is okay because of this service."

David closed the binder.

"I'm not asking you to change the rules. I'm asking you to follow your own logic. If it's legal for a doctor to care for a stranger by phone in a hospital, then it's legal for us to do it with more accountability and better tools."

Silence.

Then murmurs from the other Board members.

Dr. Angela Morris, a soft-spoken internist with twenty years in practice, leaned into her mic. "Mr. Watson is correct. We've allowed cross-coverage for decades. What VirtuCare is doing is more robust than most coverage protocols."

Crane leaned forward, cold and deliberate. "This Board does not answer to the marketplace. We answer to the safety of patients. And this model, unchecked, will cause harm."

Doctor Benjamin Falstaff replied evenly. "And so could outdated regulations that delay access to care."

Crane was clearly angry about the turn of tide, and knew that the Board would not see his insistence as reasonable.

A vote was called.

Crane and five others voted no.

Fourteen members voted yes.

Two abstained.

The motion passed.

VirtuCare was cleared to continue operations under a formal regulatory review process. No shutdown. No criminal referrals.

* * *

Byron met David at the steps with a stunned look.

"They overruled him," Byron whispered. "They actually overruled Benedict Crane."

David looked out at the line of reporters forming near the sidewalk.

"This was never about loopholes," he said. "It was about truth. And truth has a funny way of surviving fire."

Byron clapped him on the back. "Spoken like a man who just walked out of Thermopylae."

David smiled. "Except this time, the Spartans won."

6

The Battle Begins

After all of the reporters, witnesses, and members of VirtuCare left the room, Benedict Crane stood, scowled at the members who had voted against him, and shoved his chair back with such force that it skidded, squealing across the marble floor. His face was a mask of restrained fury.

"I don't know how in the hell you came to that dangerous decision, but now a crosshair will be squarely on this Board, my Board, when people start to die from telemedicine," Crane lectured with brows furrowed.

Most of the Board members avoided his gaze. A few even shifted awkwardly in their seats, ashamed, or perhaps relieved that they hadn't sided with him.

Crane didn't bother with pleasantries. He stormed out of the chamber, ego bruised and boiling over with anger.

In his office, he slammed the door and ripped off his glasses, hurling them onto his desk. The fury clouded his vision as he began to think through how he would stop this travesty so the inevitable deaths would not be attributed to his term as Director of the Board.

"What the hell are they teaching doctors these days? Are they so blinded by technology that they cannot remember how to practice medicine?" he uttered to no one in the room but himself.

He then poured himself a glass of scotch and stared at the diploma on his wall. Professor Malor wouldn't have let this happen if it was his watch.

That was it. Victor Malor had always been a great influence and ally.

He reached for the phone and punched in an old number that he had memorized long ago.

"Hello," the elderly voice answered.

"Professor Malor?"

"Hello, Crane," the elderly voice greeted his protégé. "How are things on the bureaucratic side of medicine?"

"Sir," Crane growled. "They overruled me. The Board voted to let VirtuCare continue their telemedicine operations. They didn't even bring lawyers, just a pile of nonsense about how telemedicine is improving cross-coverage care. Their CEO cited a legal precedent where this type of care was ruled as a legal standard."

"Well, that was a clever move." Dr. Victor Malor replied, Crane pictured him from the other side of the phone rubbing his chin thoughtfully. The once-powerful dean, now retired, spent most of his time reading for entertainment. On this particular afternoon, he was already sipping scotch in his home study in Connecticut, which was filled with shelves of medical tomes and legal briefings.

"It caught me off guard," Crane admitted.

"How did you react after the vote?"

"I was pissed," he explained. "I told them their decision would kill people and I stormed out of there."

"Son, if you're going to play politics, you're gonna need to not let things get under your skin. You've got to be cold, methodical, and learn to keep the majority on your side."

Benedict Crane thought about his mentor's advice, "So, what now?"

"You pushed too hard on the front door, Benedict. First, you need to get the Board members back on your side. Swallow your pride and apologize."

"Okay," he agreed, but hated the thought.

"Next, you need to be more surgical. You are a surgeon, not a wrecking crew. Think scalpel, not sledgehammer."

Crane thought about the advice and hated it. "They're practicing medicine without presence. A physician who has never touched the patient, often times in a different state, just makes a phone call and they call that care! It's a mockery, and a violation of everything we were trained to do."

"Of course it is," Malor agreed. "But the public doesn't see it that way. They see speed and convenience. They've all heard the story of Darren Lake and his damn cardiac stent and think all cases will turn out that way."

Crane nearly growled. "So, what do I do? Sit on my hands while they rewire medicine into a call center?"

There was a pause on the line.

"Become the surgeon, but bleed them," Malor said. "Help uncover the paper cuts, Benedict. Go after their physicians. Hit them with individual licensing reviews, ethics board referrals, and malpractice suspicions. Everyone has done something wrong at one point or another. Dig those somethings up."

"Right," Crane was beginning to see a pathway.

"They rely on doctors working with multiple state licenses, and call it Super Doc, as if it gives their physicians some superpower," Malor continued. "Stall their Super Doc applications so they can't keep up with growth. That will cause them to begin making mistakes or taking risks, and we will have a microscope on them the whole time, watching every move they make."

"We?"

"Yes, we," Malor answered. "You called me for help, so hire me as a consultant. Let me help you!"

Benedict Crane was now beaming, "The great Victor Malor is coming out of retirement to serve as a consulting advisor to the Federal Board of Medical Examiners. I love it!"

"Thanks, son. I've become bored with the political thrillers, honey dos, and afternoon scotch."

"What do you think about engaging the support of the large insurance companies?" Crane offered. "They can't be happy about a service that only charges $35 and gets quack doctors to patients in minutes."

"Now you're using the brains that made you my number one student, Benedict. Start whispering into the ears of insurers. Tell them a federal ruling against telemedicine is imminent. Fear coupled with revenue will drive decisions at the highest level."

Crane's silence lasted a beat too long.

"Are you up for that, Benedict?" Malor urged.

"Oh," Crane replied, with a voice that resonated with confidence, "I'm not just up for it. I'm going to make VirtuCare wish they never filed incorporation papers."

* * *

The following morning, Crane called Doctor Jeremey Falstaff, the longest standing member of the Board, and one of the members who had voted 'yes' for VirtuCare.

"Good morning, Doctor Falstaff. It's Crane."

"What can I do for you, Doctor Crane?" Falstaff asked suspiciously.

"I just wanted to apologize for my behavior yesterday. I slept on it and have made a couple of important realizations."

"Okay," Falstaff responded flatly, then paused to listen.

"I think maybe you were right. We should give VirtuCare a chance. Let's watch them and see how it progresses."

Falstaff was shocked by the comment but knew Crane's reputation as one of the most brilliant and driven young doctors in the country. "I'm relieved and not surprised to hear that, Crane. What's the other realization?"

"I brought my ego into the room and got angry. I'm embarrassed I allowed that to happen and sincerely apologize. I plan to call each of the other Board members to do the same."

"You have a great reputation, Doctor Crane. It appears our confidence in you as an exceptional Director will pay off. Thank you for your humble position. We all make mistakes, but it is generally the great ones who learn from those mistakes. In any case, let me know how I can support you moving forward."

"Thank you, Doctor Falstaff. I appreciate your confidence."

Benedict lightly set the phone on its cradle, smiled, and muttered, "What a sucker." He repeated the call with each and every Board member.

Now, for the next step in the plan: clandestine, restrained operations, executed with patience.

When Victor Malor arrived at the Board HQ in D.C. two days later, he suggested hiring private detectives to dig up dirt on the VirtuCare doctors.

"We cannot pay for that," Benedict responded with a bit of shock.

"You are correct that the Board cannot," Malor nodded. "I will fund it. I owe a great deal of wealth and a lifetime of satisfaction to the medical profession, so I view it as a good investment to protect it going forward. I have a service that knows how to be discrete," he winked at Benedict.

"Understood," Crane acknowledged. "On a related note, I have scheduled a private conference call under the alias *'Policy Integrity Briefing – FBME Regulatory Advisory.'* Three of the largest insurance carriers have agreed to join the call."

"When is it?"

Crane looked at his watch, "In about twenty minutes."

The virtual boardroom opened with a click.

Crane punched in from his office, with Malor listening in on speaker phone. He intentionally adjusted his tone to something measured but ominous.

"Thank you all for joining. I'll keep this brief. Since assuming the role as director of the Federal Board of Medical Examiners, I have been reviewing innovations and policy to make sure our care system continues to improve, while also staying safe. We are in the final stages of reviewing a legal ruling that will likely declare the current model of telephonic and interstate virtual care non-compliant with federal standards. While we acknowledge significant value for the internet and for the growing telecom services in general, we believe it is not an appropriate platform for the practice of medicine."

The head of Horizon Care, a slick executive with gray temples and an MBA cadence, leaned forward. "You're talking about VirtuCare, and some of the other startups following in their wake, I assume?"

"I'm not naming names," Crane said, steepling his fingers. "But generally, companies that are enabling physicians to treat patients they have never touched, or even across state lines, would be subject to the new rulings. Their claims may soon be deemed invalid. From your chair, it would make reimbursement, well, uhhh, let us say, risky."

A younger exec from Guardian Health frowned. "Are you saying we're going to be liable for reimbursing illegal medical services?"

"I'm saying," Crane replied, voice now a thin blade, "that if you continue to reimburse those claims without reevaluation, your shareholders could be exposed. Class-action exposed. This Board will not shield payors that knowingly ignore emergent federal policy."

The telephone connection was dead silent.

The attending legal counsel for Provident Care chimed in. "So, can you be specific? What are you recommending?"

"Simple," Crane said. "I suggest you pause any integration or expansion plans with telehealth providers operating across state lines.

Begin internal audits of claims related to such services. And if you're asked about any company with a remote business model, including VirtuCare, say you are re-evaluating participation pending legal clarification. That buys you time. And it sends a message."

* * *

The following morning, Crane paced in his office that now looked more like a litigation bunker. Legal pads, statutes, binders, and ethics codes were strewn across the table. Victor Malor reclined in a chair studying a three-year-old case while two assistants waited nervously.

"Here's how this plays out," Crane announced. "We are opening independent investigations on twelve VirtuCare physicians. Start with their cross-coverage records. I want to see every call log, every diagnosis, every prescription. Flag them for review."

"But sir," one assistant stammered, "some of these doctors have clean records. No complaints, no errors, and no med mal."

Crane turned, eyes sharp. "Do you know the best way for us to protect our healthcare system? We have to be diligent; catch things before they happen, and keep them on their toes. If their practice is like a house of cards, we can't wait for the entire thing to come down on unsuspecting patients. We cannot allow the whole structure to collapse under its own illusion of stability."

He snapped his fingers. "And freeze all pending SuperDoc licensing requests tied to VirtuCare or its affiliates. We need to take some time for further review. Doctors licensed in dozens of states make me very nervous. If nothing else, it's a matter of public safety."

The assistant scribbled furiously.

Crane walked to the window and looked out over the D.C. skyline. His reflection stared back at him in the glass, grim and unyielding.

When the assistants left the room, he looked at professor Malor, "They think they've won," he uttered, grinning, "but the siege has just begun."

* * *

Klark Thomas walked through the automatic doors of the building where VirtuCare had just moved headquarters in Addison, Texas. The reality of what Byron and his team had built suddenly hit Klark. For over three decades he had traveled the world planting seeds, and this one had grown into a real powerhouse that was beginning to make real waves. The feeling only grew as he toured the facilities and looked at the humming servers and the chatter of young engineers clustered around glowing screens. It felt like stepping onto the bridge of a starship that he'd helped blueprint but never expected to see soar.

Byron Cook looked up from a conference table littered with printouts and empty coffee cups. He stood, straightening his ever-present tie, and gave Klark a cautious nod. "I thought you'd retired to the land of skeptics and conference circuits," Byron teased, voice as dry as Texas in August.

Klark grinned, "Couldn't resist seeing if you'd turned this into another committee meeting hellscape," he looked around the room, then down the long hallway. "Honestly, Byron, this is impressive. You've advanced from video carts at correctional facilities, to dial tones, to, well," he waved at the glass walls and sleek tablets, "to mission control."

Byron allowed himself a rare, tight smile. "It took all of my hair," he touched his now bald head, "and more patience than I could single-handedly muster, but I agree that we've done well. What I came to realize is that it really takes a combination of skills. Innovation along with an understanding of how care delivery works is not enough. I needed to bring someone else in to run the business side of the show."

As if on cue, David Watson entered the room, energy in his stride and a legal pad already open in his hands. He stuck out his hand. "The legendary Doctor Klark Thomas. What an honor to finally meet you." His handshake was firm, eyes bright with curiosity.

"Just call me Klark," he waved away the formality. "I hear you're the guy who thinks every problem has a solution?"

"That's probably because I've broken everything in the learning process," David laughed. "In any case, welcome home, Klark. I've been quoting your early research for years, and I might have even stolen some of your jokes along the way."

Klark winked. "You're welcome to use any of my jokes, as long as you deliver the punchlines better than me."

The three spent the next hour tossing ideas around the whiteboard—Byron's steady pragmatism anchoring the conversation, David's relentless optimism charging the air, Klark's wit and clinical insight bridging the two. By the end, Klark felt that rare electricity of a team coming together for something bigger than themselves.

He leaned back, arms crossed, a smile tugging at the edge of his mouth. "Alright, I'm in. If you'll still have me, that is."

"In?" David asked, focused on getting clarity.

"Make me an advisor before I change my mind," Klark started, "and you two are buying dinner."

David clapped his hands. "Deal. There's a new Mexican place called El Mercado on Belt Line, about a mile up the road. Their margaritas are lethal, and the salsa is the best around. We can do a true Texas toast to new beginnings."

Klark pulled out his phone. "Mind if I invite Jennice Walters? She's been part of this telemedicine adventure since before you two could spell *modem*."

Byron and David nodded, both curious and a little amused.

A few hours later, Byron, David, Jen, and Klark found a table at the bustling El Mercado.

"Okay, so, I have read most of the early reports and papers from the early days of telemedicine," David started. "I recognize Nurse Walter's name…"

"It's now Doctor Walters," Klark corrected.

"Congrats on surviving med school," David grinned, took a chip, and scooped a sizeable helping of salsa.

"Thanks, David. Survival is an appropriate term, but I do enjoy the practice."

"What I didn't realize was that the two of you were a couple," David added with a bit of speculation.

"We weren't," Klark answered, flushing slightly with embarrassment.

Jennice put her hand on Klark's shoulder and grinned. "Your observation is a good one, David. We probably should have been…but this is new, actually."

David nodded, "Understood. I can only assume that Klark was so wrapped up in changing the future that he couldn't see the opportunity right in front of him?"

Klark and Jennice turned to each other, clearly well connected…now.

"Yup, priorities were off," Klark admitted.

David Watson held up his glass. "A toast to appreciating what we have today with old friends, new faces, and the possibility that Klark finally has added some spice to the relentless pursuit of the future." He took another ship and healthy serving of salsa.

Jennice, grinning, feigned offense. "Careful, Watson. I brought my stethoscope, and I'm not afraid to use it if you keep abusing the chips, salsa, and queso like that."

Klark laughed, "Jennice's medical notes are so good, I'm convinced she's the only reason I ever looked competent."

Byron, deadpan, nodded. "It's true. Every telemedicine pioneer needs a partner who actually knows how to find a vein, and of course an afterhours location for great meals and gatherings."

Jennice wagged a finger at Byron. "And every engineer needs someone to explain that 'turning it off and on again' isn't a universally accepted treatment protocol."

"Now you're confusing me with Michelle from our IT department. Every time I call for help, the first thing she says is: have you tried rebooting?"

"Are you saying that we can't do that with hearts?"

"Only in bad marriages," Byron smirked.

The waiter arrived with a fresh round of margaritas and sizzling fajitas. "Careful," he warned, "the plates are hotter than Texas asphalt in July."

Klark didn't miss a beat. "Thanks, amigo, but you should see the temperature in a hospital break room when someone microwaves fish."

Jennice groaned. "Now I know you really *are* a doctor. No one else would traumatize us with that memory."

Byron grinned, watching the banter. "I'm starting to feel like I'm at a comedy roast, not a business dinner."

Over the course of the next two hours, the table was nonstop stories, laughter, and plans to use telemedicine to change the world.

But as the plates emptied and the noise from the bar dimmed, Byron leaned in, his voice lowering. "Alright, fun's over. We need to talk about the elephant in the room."

"To what elephant do you refer, Doctor Cook?" Klark asked.

"Benedict Crane," Byron took a deep breath and exhaled slowly as he watched the energy deflate from the table. "The Federal Board isn't just sending angry letters anymore."

Klark's expression sobered. "I heard Crane's got the Board ready to go after companies crossing state lines. What's our legal footing?"

David tapped the table, the jovial mood completely gone. "I think we are good on the interstate front. All consults are handled by physicians licensed in the state where the patient is calling from.

"So, you have physician licenses in all fifty states?" Jennice asked.

"We do," David clarified. "When a patient calls in, the first thing they are asked is where they are. That way, even if the patient's home is in Ohio, she will talk to a Florida licensed provider when in Miami."

"So, what's the issue?" Klark asked.

"Crane is on a crusade to stop telemedicine," Byron responded in a solemn tone. "He's fixated on us and is lobbying to make an example out of VirtuCare. He's telling the insurance companies that the Board is drafting language to criminalize remote diagnosis unless the doctor and patient are in the same zip code."

Jennice frowned. "That's not just anti-telemedicine. Hell, it's anti-patient. People will lose access, and the Board should know it."

"Yup, the Board should know it," Byron nodded. "The problem is that we are a target. Not sure why Crane has it out for us, but he does, and it's concerning. I'm not a risk taker, but I don't know how to stop him from undoing everything we've built."

"Benedict has declared war, but I suggest we refuse to fight back," David recommended.

"How's that?" Byron asked.

David squared his shoulders and sat up, pushing away the half empty basket of chips. "No lawyers. We show the data, engage thought leaders, make friends everywhere, and keep a smile. Of course, we put patients first and inspire them to support us. If Crane wants a fight, he picked the wrong dinner table."

Jennice was nodding. "It's brilliant. It might even work."

David smiled, just a hint of the earlier mischief in his eyes. "So, you can see why we needed you back, Klark."

"Oh I see, David," Klark smirked. "You need someone who knows the stakes and isn't afraid to tell the emperor he's got no clothes."

"That just gave me the jitters," Byron shook his shoulders and frowned. "I have no interest in seeing Benedict Crane with no clothes."

"Let's discuss that one later, Klark," Jennice winked affectionately then reached for her glass. "To VirtuCare, stubbornness, and to never letting a bureaucrat stop a good idea."

The glasses clinked with a bit of resolve.

7

Lawyers, Guns, and Money

VirtuCare physician Doctor Corey Rogers sat nervously in the austere, wood-paneled hearing room of the Federal Board of Medical Examiners in Arlington, Virginia. The heavy seal of the Board loomed above the dais, a bald eagle grasping a caduceus in its talons, the Latin phrase *"Lex Medicinae Supremus Est"* carved ominously into the wood beneath it.

Corey Rogers was punctual, always early. It was a habit ingrained from his years in the navy. His wife always called it military precision. Rogers clutched a worn leather folder containing every license, every transcript, and every CME credit he'd ever earned. He had worked hard, stayed diligent, ethical, and current. By all standards, Rogers was an exemplary physician with a sterling career.

In the hearing room, he observed a half dozen physicians, each armed with attorneys who held responses inside stiff manila files. Under David Watson's recommendation, Rogers was joined by former

Surgeon General Morisoga, and no attorney.

The chair of the Licensing Oversight Subcommittee, Dr. Meredith Hall, finally entered and rapped the gavel with a crisp *crack*.

"Good morning, this hearing will now come to order," she announced. "We have fourteen cases and appeals today, so I expect everyone to be prompt in their opening statement."

Rogers watched silently as the circus began.

The first case was a tired-looking man in a rumpled gray suit who stood before the Board.

"Dr. Kendry," Hall read coldly, "You've had six medical malpractice claims filed against you in the past twenty-four months, ranging from a misdiagnosed stroke to a failed minor surgery. I can see from the file that you're not making any friends in the community."

Kendry cleared his throat. "None of the cases resulted in disciplinary findings. Three were settled by my insurance carrier, and the others are still pending."

A balding board member with thick glasses raised an eyebrow. "Would you say your clinical judgment has improved?"

"I've taken two additional diagnostics courses and hired a peer review consultant."

Hall returned to her initial position, "Doctor Kendry, your file is full of comments from people you have, well, pissed off. This Board recognizes that people make mistakes, but doctors should be caregivers. Have you looked up that word—care?"

"Yes ma'am. I am working on that, and for the record, my wife agrees with you."

Several members of the Board laughed.

After a brief sidebar with counsel, Hall nodded. "Your license reinstatement is granted. Effective immediately. Try not to make us regret this."

The next man, Dr. Louden Briggs wore a silk tie and had a permanent tan. He stepped forward confidently.

"Dr. Briggs, we note here that you wrote multiple prescriptions for opioids in your wife's name."

Briggs smiled thinly. "She had post-op pain. We were between physicians. I kept detailed notes and followed all dosage protocols."

Dr. Kendall, a Board member with a stern expression, leaned in. "But you're aware prescribing narcotics to a family member is a violation of federal and state code?"

"Yes, ma'am. I accept full responsibility."

The room was quiet for a moment. Then Hall sighed. "License reinstated with a one-year probation. Quarterly reviews."

Briggs grinned and nodded with mock humility.

A tall man with a sunken expression and nervous eyes then approached. The room felt tense.

"Dr. Stone," Hall's voice cut through the silence. "Your case involves exchanging prescriptions for sexual favors from multiple female patients."

A muffled gasp came from the back of the room.

Stone's voice trembled. "Those claims were fabricated. Two of them have since recanted."

"And the others?"

Stone lowered his eyes. "Settled. Confidentiality clauses prevent me from elaborating."

To Rogers's shock, after ten minutes of tortured legal wrangling and a statement from Stone's attorney invoking "lack of criminal conviction," the Board granted Stone a license renewal, pending six months of counseling and supervised practice.

Rogers shifted in his seat, almost nauseous. If *this* passed muster, surely his application would be a formality.

"Next, Dr. Corey Rogers, requesting reinstatement and reciprocal license approval for the state of Arkansas."

Rogers stood tall, clutching his file like a shield. "Madam Chair, I've been a board-certified internist for seventeen years. My record is clean. I've volunteered in underserved populations across three states, and for the last two years, I've been practicing telemedicine full-time through VirtuCare."

Hall didn't smile.

A lanky man at her left, Dr. Benedict Crane, cleared his throat. "Doctor

Rogers, do you perform physical exams during these virtual consultations?"

"When clinically indicated, I refer patients to in-person visits. But most cases are just routine infections, medication refills, chronic condition check-ins, and other similar situations. Those can be managed remotely with proper documentation and patient guidance."

Crane's eyes narrowed. "But you acknowledge that you do not physically examine your patients in most encounters?"

Rogers hesitated. "That's correct, Doctor Crane. That's the nature of telemedicine. The standard of care is met through other—"

"You may stop there," Crane interrupted. "The Board finds that your practice does not conform to the established code of medical delivery as defined in the Arkansas state charter."

Hall looked at Crane quizzically. It was not standard procedure to make a ruling without discussion, but Crane was Chairman. She waited to see if he was going to say anything else, but when he didn't, she stepped in. "Accordingly, your application for reciprocal licensure is hereby denied."

Rogers blinked. "Wait, denied? I am a Board-certified physician with no med mal, and my patients love me. I have served this country and volunteered, not only in my own community, but I frequently travel to provide care—free of charge for those who cannot afford it. I have difficulty understanding this ruling after the cases I just witnessed."

Crane's voice was low, calculated. "Telemedicine is not real medicine,

Dr. Rogers. Not in this forum."

Hall rapped the gavel. "Hearing concluded."

As the others filed out, Rogers remained standing, stunned. Three men with mountains of scandal had walked out with their careers intact. Yet he, who had served thousands via safe and effective remote care, had been branded illegitimate.

How was this possible, he thought?

Outside, as the doors closed behind him, Rogers muttered the words of an old Warren Zevon song: *"Send lawyers, guns, and money, dad, get me out of this…"*

* * *

When Doctor Rogers reported back to VirtuCare HQ in Addison, David consoled him, then told him to not let it bother him. He had not been written up, just refused a license, which would have been his 27th state medical license.

Grudgingly, Rogers acquiesced and walked down the hall to where Jennice was waiting to meet with him.

Klark Thomas arrived at the VirtuCare offices a few minutes later, his signature wry smile and a steaming coffee in hand. The Dallas heat hadn't deterred him; if anything, it seemed to energize him. As he pushed through the glass doors, he spotted Jennice in the conference room, already deep in conversation with Doctor Rogers and a younger woman who looked strikingly familiar.

"Klark!" Jennice called out, waving him in. "Perfect timing."

He strolled in, giving her a warm hug. "Always happy to spend time with the first lady of telemedicine."

Jennice rolled her eyes playfully, then gestured to her guest. "Klark, I'd like you to meet my daughter, Doctor Mary Cohen."

Mary stood and extended a firm handshake. "Dr. Thomas, it's an honor. I've heard about you my entire life."

Klark returned the handshake, studying her confident, sharp-eyed smile with an unmistakable spark of curiosity and purpose. "And I see the apple didn't fall far from the tree. What's this I hear about you joining the fight?"

Jennice smiled proudly. "Mary just finished her residency at the Medical College of Virginia. Top of her class. She's serving in the Air Force Reserves and volunteers with a free clinic two days a week."

Rogers nodded, "I was a Navy man, myself."

"Navy is good, Doctor Rogers," Mary grinned, eyes sparkling, "but I have time, and I want in. I've grown up hearing about the battles and breakthroughs of telemedicine. My heart is right here."

Rogers studied Mary, but didn't say anything.

"I believe in what you are doing and I want to be on the front lines," She glanced between Doctor Thomas and Doctor Rogers. "I'd prefer to be working for the company that started it all."

Before Klark could respond, the door opened again and David Watson swept in, all energy and purpose. He stopped short when he saw the trio of Klark, Jennice, and Mary.

"Well, looks like I missed the introductions," David grinned. "I'm guessing you're Mary?"

"Yes, sir." Mary shook his hand. "Doctor Mary Cohen."

"David Watson. Don't call me sir. Unlike you and Doctor Rogers, I'm not military," David quipped. "But I am very glad to meet you. We could use more warriors in this battle."

Mary laughed. "That's exactly what I came to do."

Klark settled into a chair. "So, tell us, Dr. Cohen, what's your specific interest in VirtuCare?"

Mary leaned forward, her tone passionate but measured. "Because Doctor Cook was a visionary who turned what Doctor Thomas and my mom imagined years ago into reality. You've proven what others said was impossible. And now, I believe we can take it further than anyone dreamed. More access, better outcomes, lower costs. We can quickly deliver care to patients who need us most."

Doctor Rogers glanced at Jennice, pride radiating from her eyes, then he looked at David. "What do you think?"

David smiled. "I think we'd be lucky to have her."

Jennice added softly, "And I think my daughter is exactly the kind of next-gen provider we need."

Rogers turned back to Mary. "Welcome aboard, Doctor Cohen. You're hired, but fair warning, we're in for a fight."

Mary's grin widened. "Good. I grew up with this and believe it is a fight worth engaging in."

Rogers laughed, admiring the tenacity and spunk of this new recruit. He quickly glanced at her left hand, noting the lack of a wedding ring. "Let's get to work, Doctor Cohen."

* * *

VirtuCare Chief Revenue Officer Gary Jefferson stepped out of his cab and walked up the steps to the soaring glass atrium of Universal Healthcare's Chicago headquarters, adjusting the cuffs of his crisp Brioni suit. At six foot two, with a staggering knowledge of healthcare, movie-star features, and a smile that could disarm a room, Gary had built a career out of making impossible deals happen.

Inside the elevator, he straightened his tie, checked his reflection once, and thought: *Today's the day. This is going to be the contract that puts VirtuCare on the national stage.*

Universal was the third-largest private payer in the country. If Gary could close this deal, it would give VirtuCare a solid nationwide platform and propel telemedicine past the tipping point.

He stepped off on the 33rd floor and was greeted warmly by Universal's assistant VP of operations, then escorted to a sleek conference room overlooking the Chicago skyline.

A few minutes later, Robert Monroe, Executive VP of Network Strategy and one of the most influential men in U.S. healthcare contracting, entered the room. The two men had known each other for years, having played countless rounds of golf and shared more than a few bourbon-soaked dinners at industry events.

"Gary," Monroe greeted him, clasping his hand. "Always good to see you."

"Robert," Gary grinned. "I appreciate you making time. I think we both know VirtuCare is exactly what your members need."

Monroe didn't smile back. Instead, he gestured toward the chair. "Sit."

Gary's instincts prickled. Something was off, but he kept the smile. "Hope you had a good weekend?"

Monroe's tone was clipped. "Let's get to it."

Gary opened his portfolio, sliding a polished proposal across the table. "Robert, our service metrics are unmatched. We are seeing ninety-seven percent patient satisfaction, response times under twelve minutes, and documented savings per member per year."

Monroe cut him off. "I know all this, Gary. I've read every slide. The problem isn't your numbers. It's that this isn't going to happen. Not here at Universal, and frankly, not anywhere."

Gary blinked, stunned for a beat. "I'm sorry, what?"

Monroe leaned back. "I had a briefing this morning with representatives from the Federal Board of Medical Examiners. They made it very clear. Telemedicine, as currently practiced, is about to be ruled noncompliant. The Director, Doctor Benedict Crane, all but told us that companies like yours will be declared illegal within months."

Gary's jaw tightened. "Robert, you and I both know that's political noise. There is no statute banning what we do. In fact, we're working hand-in-hand with regulators, the Surgeon General and two former HHS Secretaries."

"You don't get it," Monroe interrupted, voice rising. "It's not about what's legal today. It's about what will be legal six months from now. We cannot risk tying the Universal name, our shareholders, and our revenue stream to a platform that's going to be labeled non-compliant."

Gary's tone sharpened. "So, you're letting fear dictate your strategy? You and I have known each other a long time. I thought you were a leader."

Monroe's expression darkened. "Careful, Gary."

"I *am* being careful, Robert, and you're wrong about this. Your members want this. The employers want this. They all *need* this and are crying for it." Gary took a breath and looked out the window towards Lake Michigan. "You're going to throw it away because Benedict Crane is whispering in your ear?"

"Doctor Crane runs the Federal Board, Gary."

"He doesn't write the laws and the tide is turning against him."

Monroe shook his head, motioned to a man standing in the hallway and stood. "You need to leave, Gary."

"Are you serious?" Gary said, rising slowly. "We're here to help people. You know that."

A security officer appeared quietly at the door.

Monroe's voice dropped an octave. "Out of respect for our history, I'm giving you one chance to walk out gracefully. Do not put me in a position to escalate this matter."

Gary looked at Monroe with cool disbelief. Then he gathered his binder, tucking it under one arm.

"You're making a mistake," Gary said, voice measured but ice cold. "You can shut me out today, Robert. But this tide is not going to stop. And one day soon, your members are going to ask why you left them in the past."

Without waiting for a reply, Gary strode past the guard and out of the room, his pulse hammering.

As the elevator doors closed behind him and he walked into the lobby, he dialed David Watson.

"They're folding, David," Gary said, voice tight. "Universal just tossed me out of the building. Crane's poison is spreading."

On the other end, David was silent for a long moment.

Eventually David's voice broke the silence, "Get back here. We've got a war to plan."

Three days later, Rogers and Gary were in David's office along with Cook and Klark. The five of them were planning how to deal with the Board pushback to SuperDoc, and the pressure they were putting on payers, when a process server arrived to serve Doctor Rogers, again…

* * *

Two weeks later, Doctor Corey Rogers once again stood before the imposing seal of the Federal Board of Medical Examiners. In spite of the prep work, his heart was pounding a little harder than usual. The last hearing had left him reeling. He could still feel the sting, but this time he had spent more time getting prepared, and he brought David.

The room was packed with the entire Board attending in person. David Watson sat quietly in the gallery, while Byron, Klark, Jennice, and Doctor Mary Cohen all waited in the lobby, watching the hearing on the TV provided.

At the center of the Board sat Benedict Crane, cold, determined, and unreadable.

Dr. Meredith Hall banged the gavel once. "We will now hear testimony regarding the use of cross coverage in the VirtuCare model. Dr. Rogers, you may proceed."

Rogers stood tall. "Madam Chair, members of the Board. Cross-coverage is the long-established practice whereby a physician arranges for another qualified doctor to provide care to patients when the primary physician is unavailable. It allows continuity of care, ensures patient access, and prevents dangerous delays. The covering physician may be in an office with access to the patient's chart, but because coverage generally happens after hours, the covering physician is typically at home with a pager and a telephone. That does not take away from the fact that he or she is responsible for the quality of care rendered."

He glanced briefly at David, who nodded in encouragement.

Rogers continued. "Cross-coverage is a cornerstone of modern medicine. In its current form, we have been doing it since the invention of the telephone. It protects both the physician and the patient. Without it, doctors would be forced to work twenty-four hours a day, and patients would suffer dangerous lapses in care."

Several Board members nodded.

Crane's voice cut through the room. "No one here is disputing that cross-coverage is accepted. But let us be precise, Dr. Rogers. In *traditional* cross-coverage, the *primary physician* designates who covers. The patient does not select the covering doctor. Wouldn't you say that is correct?"

Rogers didn't flinch. "That is correct, in traditional practice."

"And in the VirtuCare model?" Crane pressed, leaning forward.

"In our model," Rogers replied steadily, "the patient initiates contact. When their primary physician is unavailable, the VirtuCare system matches them to an appropriate, licensed, and credentialed covering physician, who has full access to their medical record and is backed by malpractice coverage."

Crane's brow darkened. "In other words, the patient chooses their own coverage. Not the doctor."

A murmur rippled through the Board.

Dr. Hall intervened, her voice calm but pointed. "Doctor Rogers, do you understand why some might view that as a significant deviation from established standards?"

Rogers held his ground. "I understand the concern, Madam Chair. But ultimately, the goal of cross-coverage is access to safe, timely care. Whether the covering doctor is assigned by a scheduling office or chosen via a platform, the purpose is continuity, access, and patient well-being. In addition, the traditional coverage model breaks down when a patient is traveling outside their normal state of residence. VirtuCare will always deliver a doctor licensed to practice wherever the patient happens to be"

Crane's voice rose. "Enough of this nonsense about travel. Our mandate is quality of care, Doctor Rogers. This Board is tasked with ensuring standards of care are upheld, not weakened by the technological *shortcuts* your company is trying to impose on our system. You are blurring a line that has existed for generations."

Rogers opened his mouth to respond, but Crane waved him to silence.

"We believe in a physician's ability to designate a covering physician, but we do not believe the patient is capable or should be permitted to select a covering doctor when the primary is not available."

Rogers swallowed hard, watching the Board nod in agreement to the comments made by Benedict Crane.

A discussion began amongst the Board members, and it was clear they were in agreement with Crane's assessment.

Meredith Hall tapped her gavel to end the discussion, "I think we have enough data to call for a vote."

David Watson rose from his seat, his voice ringing through the chamber. "Madam Chair, may I speak?"

Hall hesitated, then nodded. "The Chair will recognize Mr. Watson. Please proceed."

David approached the podium, composed but unmistakably passionate. "Ladies and gentlemen of the Board. You've heard the mechanics of our model. Let's talk about why it matters."

He looked each member in the eye.

"In America, patients have the right to choose their doctor. That's foundational. It is a freedom that we all accept. It is a right that patients *demand*!" He emphasized. "No regulation should deny them the ability to select care when they need it most." He paused. "What is cross-coverage at its heart? It's a tool designed to serve patients and physicians alike. In our model, it still does exactly that. The covering physician is qualified. They always have full access to the medical record. This means they have a tool for diagnosis that a covering physician does not have. In addition, they have the ability to update that patient's record, which is critical for continuity of care. In our model, the covering physician is compensated, and insured. The fact is, full time VirtuCare doctors make more money than primary care physicians running a practice. On top of that, the patient receives care in minutes, rather than days, *and* pays less!"

David stopped to study the faces of each Board member. "All of these things add up, but today, you are contemplating voting on a proposal that would steal an American citizen's right to select a doctor," he paused for effect. Is that what you want to do? And if it is, please ask yourself, does that decision even belong in this room? It seems to be one more appropriate for the Halls of Congress, or the Supreme Court."

Crane's eyes narrowed, lip curling. "This is not about rights, Mr. Watson. It is about maintaining clinical standards and physician judgment. Not handing over the sacred duty of coverage to consumer choice."

David's gaze didn't waver. "With all due respect, Director Crane, patients *do* have a right to choose. And VirtuCare's model improves the system for everyone. We deliver care in under fifteen minutes. Our covering doctors are not in the dark. They know exactly who they're treating, and our outcomes are among the best in healthcare."

David paused. "VirtuCare boasts a ninety-seven percent patient satisfaction. That's more than thirty percentage points higher than almost anything else in American healthcare today."

A wave of murmured agreement swept the room.

David pressed on. "So, let me ask this Board directly: Are we here to protect outdated procedure, or are we here to protect patients? Because VirtuCare is protecting patients. We're helping doctors, and we're helping the system. To date, no telemedicine practice has had a bad outcome and no medical malpractice claims have been made on a telemedicine consultation. These are significant statistics."

He let the words hang in the air.

Dr. Hall leaned forward, thoughtful. "Mr. Watson raises an important question."

Crane, face flushed, shot back. "You would let the marketplace dictate the standards of medicine? Watson and his cronies at VirtuCare are asking that we reduce clinical practice to online reviews and digital shopping carts!"

David held his ground. "We're not reducing anything, Director Crane. We're elevating care with faster access, better documentation, improved outcomes, more compensation for providers, and higher approval ratings from the people who matter most, the patients. *That* is the future."

An uneasy silence followed.

Finally, Dr. Hall called for discussion.

For the next twenty minutes, Board members debated heatedly. Some of those members agreed with Crane's purist view, others echoed Watson's pragmatism.

When the vote was finally called, Crane's jaw was locked tight.

The tally came in: eleven to eight.

VirtuCare and Dr. Rogers were cleared to continue operating under the current model. No sanctions. No restrictions. The motion passed.

Crane's face was stone as Hall gaveled the session closed.

David exhaled and clapped Rogers on the back. "Well done, Corey. You stood tall."

Rogers let out a long breath. "It was clearly tuning against us until you stood up and became Benjamin Franklin on the floor, David. Your speech turned the tide. I honestly can't believe they sided with us."

David smiled thinly. "They sided with patients."

Across the room, Crane gathered his papers stiffly, his eyes cold as steel. For him, the battle still wasn't over.

It was just beginning.

No number of lawyers, guns, and money could stop Benedict Crane from protecting healthcare from this supposed threat.

8

The Culture of Resilience

The sun had barely crested over the Guadalupe Mountains as the VirtuCare charter buses pulled through the wide, open gate of Big Pine Ranch. Crisp, dry air rolled down from the high peaks, fragrant with juniper and creosote. David Watson stepped off the first bus, inhaling deeply and surveyed the surroundings, this was West Texas, a world away from the pressure cookers of boardrooms and federal hearings. The air was clean, crisp, and perfect for his goal.

The trip was calculated and deliberate. Every piece had been chosen with a specific end in mind.

The ranch sprawled across thousands of acres of West Texas rangeland, its main lodge a mix of rustic beams and stone, flanked by smaller cabins that dotted the hillsides. But it wasn't the lodge or the endless blue sky that drew the eye.

The primary focus was Guadalupe Peak, standing sentinel in the distance, its massive shoulders rising nearly 9,000 feet into the clear desert sky. This mountain was Texas' highest point, and the tallest mountain east of the Rockies. Guadalupe would serve as a symbol to solidify the culture and soul of this company.

Because even after months of media scrutiny, government attacks, and near-constant resistance, he knew VirtuCare's most valuable asset wasn't the technology. What VirtuCare and the world needed was a team that understood the collective belief in what they were doing. VirtuCare was at a point where the team needed to be strong enough so that it would not falter in the chaos, the attacks, and the legal pressures.

This trip, David told himself as he shouldered his pack, *is about the people.*

The working session would take place over ten days in the big stone pavilion at the center of the ranch. David kicked off the session with a description of where they were, and he didn't sugarcoat it.

"You all know what we're up against," he said, voice cutting through the mountain stillness. "Under the leadership of Benedict Crane, the Federal Board won't stop. We can expect more attacks, more hearings, more lawsuits, and even things we cannot anticipate or plan for." He paused, sweeping his gaze across the assembled engineers, nurses, docs, and staff.

"But you need to understand and appreciate what we've built. In our lifetimes, most people never have the opportunity to change the world in a meaningful way. We have that opportunity," he took a sip of his water and studied his team. "Change is hard, and what we are doing matters. In a dozen years, you will all look back and say: I built that, but today, well, today we are under attack."

David pointed to the wall of patient stories. "That single mom in Laredo who avoided the ER because of us. That rancher in Montana who got diagnosed with early CHF because of us. That woman who forgot her birth control pills on her honeymoon…" He stopped while everyone laughed. "These aren't numbers. These are lives, they are stories, they are results! That is why we fight."

* * *

Afternoons were deliberately unstructured with daily work, email catchup, and keeping the company wheels on. In addition, employees had the opportunity to engage in hikes, horseback rides, and long talks by the firepit. It wasn't just a retreat, it was therapy. And on the third afternoon, David found himself on the grueling 8-mile trail to Guadalupe Peak with Elaine Singer.

The climb was no joke. Four miles up, four miles back, with nearly 5,000 feet of elevation gain. The sun was bright but cool, the sky cloudless, and the narrow, rocky switchbacks wound along sheer cliffs, shaded in parts by hardy pines clinging stubbornly to the rock. There was no water anywhere on the trail.

David grunted as he rounded a steep bend, sweat dripping from beneath his cap. Elaine was already waiting on a flat rock, one boot propped up, her blonde ponytail exiting the back of a tan ballcap that was slightly damp with sweat, but her eyes were still sparkling.

"Come on, boss," she teased, offering him a hand. "You're supposed to be the one leading this culture hike."

David took it, laughing between breaths. "I lead better when I'm on flat ground. I had no idea what a mountain goat you were when I agreed to this hike! Besides, these West Texas peaks aren't in the CEO job description. This one is for fun, not part of the corporate structure!"

She smirked and handed him a water bottle. "You wanted to remind us of resilience, remember?"

David took a long pull and looked out over the endless sweep of desert below. "Yeah. It fits, doesn't it?" He gestured to the trail. "This… this is what the last year has felt like. It's been relentless, sometimes brutal, and lots of false summits. But, like this hike, every step matters."

Elaine nodded, her voice quieter now. "I think the team needed this. Not just the message, but having the opportunity to get to know you in this setting. I will make sure they know how much the great David Watson struggled on this trail, sweating it out just like the rest of us."

David looked at her thoughtfully. "And you? What do you need out of this trip?"

She hesitated, then smiled, softer this time. "What I need? Hmm, I think you have been delivering exactly that… to believe again. I've worked at companies that folded when the pressure came. This one is different. It *feels* different." She glanced at him. "Because of the inspiration you bring to the table. The belief that all of us can create something that changes everything. We have the opportunity to see a David Watson who takes all the blows, figures out what he did wrong, fixes it, and won't bend."

David's eyes twinkled. "I'm too stubborn for my own good."

"Stubborn works," Elaine said. "Especially now."

They started walking again, the trail narrowing to a knife-edge ridge. Wind gusted cool across the stone. Below, the vast Chihuahuan desert stretched to the horizon.

After a while, David spoke again. "You know, sometimes… I worry." He kept his eyes on the trail. "I am concerned that all this pressure, all these fights, will wear the team down, and that somewhere, we'll lose the heart of what we've built. We need to make sure that does not happen."

Elaine stopped and touched his arm. "You won't." Her voice was certain. "Because you brought us here. Not just to fight, but to remember why we're fighting, and what we are fighting for. Everyone knows that."

David met her gaze, the weight of the last few months written in his eyes. Then a smile tugged at the corners of his mouth. "You're good at this." The conversation made him wonder about Elaine Singer. His life had been one of corporate executive, and as such, he had not taken time to understand the personal lives of the team around him.

She shrugged playfully. "Part of my job description: keeping impossible CEOs on task."

They both laughed, the sound echoing against the ancient rock. And as they rounded the final bend toward the summit, David knew this was why they were here. The goal was to climb together. The summit had been an objective that everyone else had said no to because of the level of fitness required to reach the top. While several other ViruCare employees had taken other, easier hikes, everyone understood the bigger lifetime goal was to build something that would last and forever change healthcare.

On the summit was an aluminum pyramid built as a dedication to the climbers who had made the difficult trek to the top. The two sat, ate lunch, and enjoyed the view of the desert landscape more than a mile below. When they had started the day, they had been business associates with a common goal. Now they were beginning to form a friendship.

*   *   *

That night, the ranch sky was ablaze with a billion stars of the Milky Way stretching like a painted banner across the darkness. The cool mountain air had driven the team toward the big stone-ringed firepit behind the main lodge. The ranch hand had built a fire with flames that crackled and sparks drifted upward like tiny messengers.

Blankets were draped over shoulders, boots propped on benches, and glasses of whiskey and mugs of coffee were being passed around liberally. Elaine produced a guitar and began playing songs appropriate for a west Texas ranch visit. For a little over an hour, everyone sang along, and the realization David had while on the summit began to sink in with the entire team. The goal had been to fortify an understanding of the goals, challenges, and potential. Everyone knew that when this company became a success, they would all become wealthy, but even more, they would have an impact on the lives of millions.

However, an even bigger realization came to David while sitting around the campfire; this team had become a family who could now be relied on to protect each other's backs.

He stood at the edge of the circle, silhouetted by the fire, sleeves rolled, a familiar presence among friends and warriors. His voice, when he spoke, was strong, but also intentionally low enough to make people lean in to hear him.

"You know," he began, kicking at a loose stone. "We've talked a lot these last few days about resilience, and standing strong under pressure. Sometimes, it's easy to forget what that really looks like, particularly when the Board starts throwing rocks at us."

The flames danced in his eyes. "It's easy to talk about courage in a boardroom. But out here, in the Texas desert, Elaine and I got a taste of difficult challenge climbing that mountain," he motioned towards Guadalupe Peak, silhouetted by stars. I think we've all experienced a bit of the rugged environment carved right into the land around us."

He let that hang, then smiled faintly. "This state was built on a challenge that every historian can name. It began with the Alamo."

The group grew still, more than a few heads nodding.

David continued, pacing slowly. "Those men, led by William Travis, could have surrendered. They could have walked away and lived. Santa Anna's army was huge, well provisioned and on a mission. The Alamo? Less than two hundred defenders. They knew the odds. They knew it was likely suicide."

He stopped, turning toward the circle.

"So why did they stay?" he asked quietly. "Why fight when it meant certain death?"

For a long moment, no one spoke. The fire popped, casting flickering shadows across the faces of the team.

Finally, Jennice Walters leaned forward from her seat, her voice soft but sure. "I am not a Texan, but I am a lover of history, and I have read a fair amount about the Alamo. The Alamo defenders knew what they stood for was far more important than that particular day. They knew they held the key to something much bigger," she said. "It was about what would come after."

She looked around the circle, eyes shining. "In Texas, they grow up learning what the Alamo *stood* for. It wasn't just a mission, or a fort. It was a symbol of resistance and defiance. For those original Texans the Alamo was about fighting for something bigger than themselves. At the Battle of Gonzales, the Mexican Army demanded they turn over their cannons, and the men there simply raised a flag that said *Come and Take It*. I think, like in the Alamo, they weren't really talking about a cannon. They were telling the world they would not give up what matters most. At least, not without a fight."

The group was quiet, the words sinking in.

Jennice's gaze swept across her teammates. "That's what we're doing here at VirtuCare," she continued. "We're standing on a wall, like the Alamo, and yeah, maybe we're outnumbered. Clearly the Board, and Crane, and the largest insurance companies have the bigger army," Jennice stopped again, realizing she had gotten wrapped up in the story. When she looked at the team, huddled under blankets, she saw affirmation. "We've got something they don't."

She gestured toward the fire, the stars, and the gathered circle. "We've got each other. We've got the satisfaction ratings of our patients, and we've got the knowledge that what we're doing is right. What we are doing may be breaking with the status quo, but we're making healthcare better, faster, and more accessible. We're not giving that up. Not now. Not ever."

Her voice softened, but her words cut through the night. "If they want to take that away, then we should raise our own Texas flag and let them know, they'll have to come and take it!"

A wave of quiet agreement swept the group. Jennice had clearly stated what they were all beginning to think.

Klark stood and walked over to Jennice, hugged her, and turned to the team, eyes glistening in the firelight, "Damned right!"

David watched Jennice for a long moment, then raised his mug.

"To the defenders," he said softly. "And to every wall worth standing on."

A chorus of voices echoed him:

"To the defenders."

For the first time in months, beneath that vast West Texas sky, VirtuCare's team was more than a company. They were a family, a phalanx that surrounded and protected the VirtuCare model of telemedicine.

An hour later, most of the team had drifted off toward their cabins. David remained by the firepit, sipping the last of his bourbon, watching the embers glow against the dark West Texas sky.

He heard the crunch of boots in the gravel and glanced up as Elaine Singer slid onto the bench beside him, wrapping a blanket over her shoulders.

"You're a hard man to pin down," she said softly, a smile playing on her lips.

David chuckled, swirling the glass in his hand. "I was just thinking the same about you."

"Well, for one thing, I'm not a man," she responded, "and I am not difficult to pin down."

"I stand corrected. I did not know you had musical talents, Elaine."

"In reality, my passion is in music, but I learned long ago that you cannot make money making music."

David picked up the bottle and saw there was a bit more left. "You want a shot?"

"Sure."

He poured some in a glass, handed it to her and sat for a moment, watching the fading flames. Then Elaine nudged him lightly with her shoulder. "That speech tonight was effective. It worked. The team's more solid than I've seen them. They are more solid than any team I've *ever* seen. You did what you came here to do."

David exhaled, letting the weight of that settle. "Good. We're going to need that unity when the next round of fights hit."

Elaine nodded. Then, with a glance toward the edge of the clearing, she smirked. "Speaking of unity, it looks like our star physician Doctor Rogers and young Dr. Cohen are finding plenty of it."

David followed her gaze and spotted Corey Rogers and Mary Cohen standing beneath one of the old oaks, deep in conversation, faces lit with that unmistakable warmth.

He raised a brow. "I noticed that connection yesterday."

Elaine laughed softly. "David, those two have been an item since the first day they met. You're just the last to catch on."

David grinned. "Should I be worried about team members pairing off? Creates complications."

Elaine's eyes twinkled as she pulled her blanket tighter. "Too late to stop that train. Rogers and Cohen are definitely a couple. Michelle and Derek from engineering are another one. A few of the doctors are married to each other, if you haven't noticed. And rumor has it, IT has at least two couples now." She leaned in slightly. "And then there's Klark and Jennice."

David chuckled again, shaking his head. "I guess when you build something this intense, it's bound to happen."

Elaine's smile softened. "It is. You put people in a mission-driven company, high stakes, long hours, and all of the things that go with that intensity blend together. It's human nature. They connect."

She hesitated for a moment, then turned a little toward him, her voice quieter. "And, for what it's worth… I've been noticing something sparking *here*," she gestured between the two of them.

David looked at her, his brow raised. "Oh?"

She held his gaze for a beat longer than usual. "Between you and me." She smiled, slightly self-conscious now. "I think there's been a little... attraction. At least on my side."

David felt his heartbeat quicken and was glad there was not enough light for her to see him blush. For a second, he wondered if she was joking with him, but looked into her eyes, saw honesty there, and let out a slow breath. "You're not wrong," he admitted. "I noticed it during the hike today."

Elaine looked down for a second, then back at him. "That's only because you are slow at seeing human chemistry. You know, you're an excellent leader with the best culture skills, but you're slow on the emotional connection category."

"You're not the first to accuse me of that," he stared into his glass, then took a sip.

"What would you like to do with this obvious connection?"

David thought about it, voice low. "Workplace romances can be tricky, problematic. Especially here. We need the team focused, not distracted."

Elaine nodded. "True. But sometimes, when something's real, it's more distracting to ignore it."

They both laughed quietly at that.

David smiled. "You've got a point, but whatever we allow to happen, it has to be with no drama. This company and our objective is too important."

Elaine grinned. "David, if I ever create drama, you have my permission to revoke my badge."

He laughed, raising his empty glass. "Deal."

They sat in companionable silence for a while longer, watching the stars, the fire dwindling to a soft glow. The unspoken understanding between them was clear. Things would proceed with no rush, and no games. Just... possibilities.

And beneath the stars of West Texas, David studied the lines and features on Elaine's face. She was remarkable and beautiful. Why had he not seen that before now? He smiled as she turned to him, eyes sparking in the remaining firelight. He realized that they both knew, the potential and possibilities mattered.

* * *

On the final afternoon of the retreat, a thunderstorm rolled into the Guadalupe mountains. Rather than hanging out around the fire pit and listening to Elaine singing and playing guitar, small groups huddled in covered areas to watch the electric tension in the air. Out beyond the silhouette of Guadalupe Peak, fast moving cumulonimbus clouds took over the afternoon sky.

Most people skipped dinner so they could watch this rare spectacle as the first rumble of distant thunder rolled through the canyon. Some of the team retreated to their cabins or the main lodge, but David lingered beneath the wide-covered veranda outside the dining hall, bourbon glass in hand, watching nature's show unfold. There was something raw about it that made him understand why ancient civilizations believed it was the gods throwing a tantrum over the desert.

Bootsteps on wood. He glanced sideways to see Elaine approaching, ponytail poking through a ball cap, khaki shorts, a t-shirt, and hiking boots. Her eyes were bright as she remarked with a soft grin. "I figured you'd be out here."

David smiled, nodding toward the horizon. "How could I miss this? Texas storms always put on a show."

Together they stood at the railing, side by side, watching as jagged bolts tore across the sky, forking deep into the mountains and distant desert. The wind picked up, flapping their shirts, slinging occasional droplets sideways beneath the covered veranda.

When the actual storm arrived at the ranch, rain sheets cascaded out of the sky like a broken dam, slamming down with sudden, furious force.

The old veranda groaned in the gusts, and the storm howled around them. Before either could react, a gust whipped under the eaves, drenching them both.

David laughed, wiping water from his face. "So much for shelter!"

Some people would have been terrified by the sudden fury of nature, but Elaine laughed, eyes sparkling. "Come on! Before we both drown."

Together, they bolted through the downpour, dodging puddles, but acquiescing to the soaking. Elaine grabbed his hand without thinking, and they ran together up the slippery path toward her cabin.

As they stumbled breathless through the door, soaked to the skin, the storm was raging full force with wind screaming against the windows and thunder shaking the walls.

David suddenly realizing he was in Elaine's cabin, looked around with water dripping onto the wooden floor. "Hell of a storm," he managed to say, while trying to think through what would happen next, or how to gracefully depart.

Elaine peeled off her outer layer, hair damp and loose around her shoulders. She grabbed a towel and tossed him one. "Dry off or you're going to catch pneumonia, boss."

David rubbed at his face and hair, grinning. "You pulled me into this, you know."

She looked up, eyes gleaming with mischief. "Yes, of course I did. Mother Nature and I worked on this plan just this morning."

He laughed, then nervously tossed the towel aside and tried to avoid her gaze. The laughter faded, the room suddenly quieter in spite of the steady pounding of rain and the occasional bang of thunder echoing off the mountains.

They stood there, breath mingling, inches apart. The moment stretched.

Then, Elaine leaned in. "That mischievous Mother Nature," she whispered.

Their lips met soft at first, but then grew deeper, more urgent. The tension that had simmered for several days finally broke, melting into warmth and hunger.

Elaine pressed closer, her hands sliding to his shoulders. David pulled her in, heart pounding, the storm outside matching the charge between them.

When they finally parted, breathless, Elaine rested her forehead against his. "Well," she whispered in a silky voice, "I guess we answered *that* question."

David smiled, his voice low. "Yeah. No more pretending."

She traced a finger lightly along his jaw. "Still worried about workplace dating policies?"

He chuckled softly. "It would seem that your friend Mother Nature has other plans for us this evening,"

Outside, the wind and storm howled on, but the real stage had shifted to the warmth of that small cabin, and outpost in the desert storm.

The following morning, the air had taken on that clean, sharp edge that only rain in the high desert can deliver. The sunrise bathed Guadalupe Peak in a blaze of gold and orange, casting long shadows across the stone courtyard where the team gathered for one last breakfast.

David stood on the wooden steps of the lodge, hands in his jacket pockets, taking in the view. Around him, laughter and conversation, expressing the clear connections that were developing. After breakfast, people packed gear, snapped photos, and swapped stories from their favorite parts of the retreat.

David Watson could feel it in the air: the trip had worked. He also clearly saw the friendships and deeper personal relationships that had developed amongst the team. The weariness and tension that had weighed so heavily back at HQ was now replaced with determination and sense of purpose.

Byron Cook appeared beside him, coffee mug in hand. "Not bad for a few days in the mountains."

David nodded. "Exactly what we needed."

Byron glanced around. "You see them? These people are ready for the fight. More ready than they were two weeks ago."

"They're the phalanx," David said softly, remembering the firepit conversation. "We hold the line. No matter what comes."

Byron sipped his coffee. "Well, let's hope Crane isn't planning to throw another army at us this week."

David gave a wry grin. "I do not understand what drives that man, but I have come to realize that he is relentless."

By late morning, the convoy of charter buses began rolling south, winding through the canyons and scrubland back toward the highways.

David sat near the front, laptop open but untouched. His thoughts kept drifting to the faces around him, doctors, engineers, admin staff, all talking, laughing, and energized. The bonds forged on those hikes and around that firepit would hold when the next wave of attacks hit.

Across the aisle, Elaine caught his eye and smiled a quiet, knowing look that said *we're ready*. David returned it with a nod.

By the time they pulled into the parking lot of VirtuCare HQ in Addison two days later, the team was buzzing with purpose.

Inside the bright glass atrium, Ruthie from the front desk greeted them with a grin. "Well, look what the desert blew back in."

David clapped his hands. "Alright, people, let's get back to work. We've got a healthcare system to fix."

Laughter echoed through the lobby, but the energy was unmistakable. The team was tighter, tougher, and more unified than ever before.

Byron sidled up beside David as they rode the elevator to the executive floor. "One hell of a retreat."

David smiled. "Yeah. Now let's see if we can keep that spirit alive."

Byron's expression grew serious. "We're going to need it. I heard Crane's pushing a new round of Board reviews. He's not done with us."

David's jaw tightened. "That man has no idea what he's up against. This isn't a passing idea, it's the beginning of a storm that will forever change the system. In any case, we'll be ready."

He looked out across the growing floor of VirtuCare's headquarters, then fixed his eyes on Elaine's office. She was rearranging something, then looked up and caught his eye. The smile didn't say I remember what we did last night, instead, it simply seemed to affirm something he clearly felt…

Byron had been admiring the dozens of desks, glowing monitors, a hive of motion and purpose when he caught the facial expression and gaze of his lifelong friend. He traced that gaze down to Elaine Singer.

"We're ready David," Byron said as he glanced between David and Elaine. "The defenders have climbed the mountain together," he winked at his friend, grinned, and walked back to his office.

* * *

A month after the retreat in West Texas saw an undeniable change in corporate culture. The attacks from the Federal Board, which had been constant and draining in the months prior, had stopped, at least for the moment. No new summons, no new hearings. Word inside the building was that Crane was biding his time, regrouping. But for now... there was room to breathe.

And with that room to breathe, the business grew, and a few other things evolved as well…

It was on a crisp Saturday night when Klark and Jennice extended an impromptu dinner invitation to Byron and David. It would be just a casual evening, they'd said.

At the last minute, Jennice emailed again: *Corey and Mary are joining us. Hope that's okay. The more the merrier.*

David grinned and shot an email back: *Of course. Looking forward to it.*

They gathered at Klark's favorite little bistro just off the Tollway. It was a place with worn wood floors, great wine, and the kind of low lighting that made the troubles of the world feel far away.

Byron was already there when David arrived, nursing a Scotch. "Still no shots fired from Crane," Byron said as David slid into the booth. "I'm starting to think he's lost his edge."

"Don't count on it," David replied. "Crane is planning and plotting. This quiet period is the calm before the storm."

A few minutes later, Klark and Jennice arrived, arm in arm, looking every bit the happy couple everyone had come to see them as.

Doctors Rogers and Cohen followed soon after, still glowing from their own newness as a couple.

Drinks were poured, appetizers passed. The conversation bounced easily, about growth, the latest system upgrades, and patients who were raving about the platform.

Then, after a round of toasts, Klark stood and cleared his throat.

"We, uhh… didn't just invite you here for the wine," he began with a sheepish grin. "We've got a bit of news."

Jennice beamed beside him.

Klark continued, "Well… we went ahead and made it official! Jen and I tied the knot last week, just us and a little ceremony at the courthouse."

Byron blinked, then grinned. "You sly old dog."

David laughed, raising his glass. "To the happy couple!"

Everyone toasted, cheers filling the little corner of the restaurant.

Then David, with a mischievous twinkle, added, "So, was this a shotgun wedding? When's the family expansion going to be announced? Got any news *there*, Klark?"

The table burst into laughter. Klark threw up his hands. "David, I'm in my late-sixties. Jennice is... well, close enough. I think we'll leave the baby-making to the younger generation."

Jennice winked. "Speak for yourself, old man! I've still got some fire left."

The group roared.

Mary then set down her glass and looked around, a shy but excited smile on her face. "Actually, we have some news too."

Corey Rogers grinned and took her hand. "We're getting married. Two months from now."

The cheers went up again, louder this time.

"We want it to be a big celebration," Mary added. "We met here, so it seems appropriate to have a VirtuCare family event."

Byron clapped him on the back. "Now *that* will be a hell of a party."

David nodded, eyes twinkling. "Count us in. Every one of us."

Doctor Rogers cocked his head, looking at David, "You haven't asked when we will be starting our family."

"Uhhh," David stumbled. "Do you have news? Is there a VirtuCare baby on the way?"

"No, not yet," Mary started, "but we were thinking maybe right after the wedding we'd like to start trying."

The entire group burst into cheers and toasts to the new couples and promising hope of the first VirtuCare baby.

As the cheers quieted, Klark glanced over at David, a playful smirk on his face. "And speaking of VirtuCare couples, how are things going with you and Elaine?"

All eyes turned.

David grinned, not missing a beat. "Things are good. Actually, more than good. She's a brilliant woman and a great partner. I'm lucky as hell to have her."

There were smiles and knowing nods all around.

Jennice lifted her glass again. "To love, in all its forms. And to this wild, wonderful family we've built."

They clinked glasses, the sound ringing warm in the night.

On this Spring evening in north Texas, there was no Federal Board, no battles, no politics. The evening was just friends, family, and a future worth fighting for.

9

The Crane Salvo

Benedict Crane stood at the window of his D.C. office, watching the light rain and its impact on traffic. The lighting in the room was just about perfectly balanced so he could also use the window as a mirror, his reflection stared back. What he saw were the cold eyes and tight jawed reflection of a man who hated losing. His righteous battle with VirtuCare had dealt him too many losses lately. It was time to turn the tides.

The Board had twice ruled in favor of VirtuCare. His push with the insurers had begun to stall under patient demand, and press resistance had shifted to support for telemedicine.

But not for long.

Crane turned back toward the room, where Victor Malor sat in an armchair, sipping tea, a thick dossier open on his lap.

"They're gaining ground," Crane said flatly. "Too many wins. Too much goodwill. If we wait too long, they'll have an avalanche of momentum, and then we'll never stop them."

Malor nodded and grinned. "So, now is the time for another hammer. What do you have in mind, son?"

Crane shook his head. "No. Not a hammer this time. Something more powerful, and surgical."

He strode to his desk and tapped the folder. "We go after the weakness that no one will tolerate and they can't defend."

"And that is?"

Crane tossed his folder on the desk, "controlled substances."

Malor's eyes gleamed. "A narcotics scandal. I like it."

"Exactly." Crane's voice was hard now. "We bait them. We catch them prescribing narcotics through that glorified call center. The public won't care about EMRs and fast response times if they believe VirtuCare is fueling the opioid crisis."

"And how do you intend to bait them?" Malor asked.

Crane's smile was thin. "We hire an actor. A professional patient with the skill to sound desperate, to cry in pain, to play on the heartstrings of experienced doctors. We have our actor patient call in repeatedly. Then we start counting up the infractions."

"I…" Malor broke in, then stopped as he rubbed his chin in thought, "Is that legal? Can we hire actors to trick the doctors?"

"We aren't technically tricking doctors, professor. What we are doing is gathering evidence and data that HIPAA would not allow us to pull otherwise. Remember, our job is to protect the system."

"Okay," Malor was not completely convinced, but Crane was making a good argument.

Crane pulled a sealed envelope from his briefcase. "And this," Crane said, tapping the envelope, "is an anonymous tip I'm sending to the DEA. Suggesting that VirtuCare is nothing more than a narcotics delivery system in disguise. They'll have eyes on every call, every script. In a criminal investigation, the DEA will be able to look at all of the files. They will provide our backup."

Malor chuckled softly. "Subtle. And if it works?"

"Then we have what we need to destroy them," Crane said coldly. "And not through the Board, which I think is tiring of my attempts to shut telemedicine down. This time, we will use the court system, and the media. All of it will be backed by federal law enforcement. Those self-righteous assholes in Texas will all find themselves behind bars. Right where they belong."

Malor nodded. "You, well, *we* are playing a dangerous game."

"It's worth the risk," Crane replied. "Because I will *not* let that company rewrite the standards of American medicine."

"Yes Crane, it's definitely worth the risk." Still, a part of Malor wondered if they weren't pushing too close to the edge.

Two weeks later Crane had selected an actor who arrived in D.C. for training. He was a talented, yet unknown, off-Broadway performer named Ray Jamison. He was in his late thirties, lean, and had a face that could swing between boyish and haunted. Mostly, he was capable and hungry for this opportunity.

Crane's team walked him through VirtuCare's technology: the app interface, the intake process, the way calls were routed. They drilled him on pain symptoms, on the language of desperation. *My doctor is on vacation. I'm allergic to NSAIDs. It's terrible, I can't sleep. The pain is unbearable. PLEASE HELP ME!*

They rehearsed the timing; when to cry, when to choke up, how to build urgency without tipping the doctors too early.

By the end of the first week, Jamison was good. Too good. Even the team's medical consultant, a retired ER doc, admitted, "He could fool anyone. Hell, I'd give him the meds!"

Crane smiled at that. "Perfect."

The calls began in week three of the planning stage. Jamison was given twenty different pseudonyms, and Crane's staff set each one of them up in the VirtuCare system, even paying the fees for setup and consultations.

Call #1: No script. Doctor escalated for in   evaluation.

Calls #2a, b, c, and d: Same patient with i   t attempts. No script. Nurse flagged the patient history for repeat patterns.

Call #3: Blocked at intake by algorithm. Referral to pain management.

Calls #4-6: Different times, different doctors. Each flagged, each denied.

Jamison adapted after each failure. Changed his story. Added more pathos. Tinkered with his presentation.

Calls #7-11: Still no success.

On the twelfth attempt, Jamison sat in a hotel room, phone in hand, frustration etched on his face.

Across the city, Crane sat in his office, reviewing the latest call reports from the DEA contact.

"Eleven times," Malor said quietly. "And not one bite."

Crane's eyes burned. "We keep going."

Malor studied him. "You may have underestimated their system."

Crane's voice turned to ice. "Then we'll escalate. Everyone has a breaking point. And I'm pretty sure I have an idea to expose theirs."

"What's that?"

"Christmas," Crane grinned. "What doctor can deny a patient in pain over Christmas?

* * *

Around the same time that Crane was training his actor, David Watson was in his office at VirtuCare HQ, in the middle of a high-level strategy session with Byron, Michelle, and two of the newer physician leads seated around his conference table. They were deep in numbers, mapping out expansion targets, when the door to David's office creaked open.

Everyone stopped talking and looked up.

Ruthie stood in the doorway, and one look at her face told David something was wrong. *Very* wrong. Ruthie never interrupted meetings. Not for anything. David was already standing by the time she crossed the threshold into the executive office.

She stepped close, her voice a tight whisper against his ear: "David… the DEA. Guns. Badges. They're here." She was trembling.

For a single heartbeat, time seemed to stop. A cold weight hit his gut. *Shit, the DEA.*

They had planned for so many things, but the DEA, with their guns and badges, had not been one of them.

David made himself calm down. Right now, he needed to be the leader everyone was expecting. He gave Ruthie's arm a quick squeeze. "Just stay calm, Ruthie. I will handle this."

In reality, he had no idea how to handle it. He then thought about something Elaine had said to him while on the mountain: *It's easier if you take it one step at a time.*

He turned to Byron and Michelle, who were already on their feet. Byron looked grave, but steady. Michelle's eyes were blazing. They both knew, no need for words.

David straightened his jacket, smoothed his cuffs, and then he opened the door.

The hallway stretched ahead, long and glass-bright, the entire company visible. And even before he stepped out, he knew, the entire floor, probably everyone in the building, already knew what waited at the gates.

Was this the Alamo? And the DEA was Santa Anna's Army?

Yet, at VirtuCare, no one was panicking.

In fact, as he walked down the hall, what struck David instantly was the stillness, steadiness, and confidence of his team.

Heads were up. Doctors at their screens. Nurses and engineers, pausing but holding their ground. No one was running, or hiding. No whispered gossip. He saw only the eyes of his phalanx, sharp, aware, and intentionally meeting his as he walked.

And in those eyes, David saw it: *resolve.*

There was fear, but no collapse. Everyone held that quiet, iron-cored confidence they had forged together out there on that West Texas mountain. Burned into their very fiber was the belief that this was a cause worth fighting for. Worth standing for.

He continued the long walk down the hallway, his gaze swept left to right, catching the small moments. Elaine was leaning against the reception counter, posture relaxed but ready. Michelle's IT leads standing at their terminals, jaws tight with purpose. Several physicians, Dr. Rogers among them, were standing openly in their glass offices, arms crossed, faces calm.

No one was hiding. No one looked like they were about to fold. This wasn't fear. This was *passionate belief in a cause*.

At the reception area, Elaine stepped beside him, matching his stride. Her voice was low and even. "They came in hard, badges out. Three of them. I met them at the door. They asked for you, but we are the phalanx. No matter what happens in there, you are not alone."

David's eyes flicked toward her, a brief smile ghosting across his lips. "You alright?"

Elaine's eyes gleamed. "More than alright. We all know this is what you were preparing us for. We are ready for this."

Together, they reached the glass-walled conference room. Three DEA agents stood inside, two men, one woman. Sidearms holstered, but prominently visible. The air inside the room was thick with self-importance. The agents were clearly trying to project authority and intimidation.

David's jaw set. *Not here. Not today.*

He paused for a beat, scanning the floor one last time.

His people were watching him. Their leader. And every pair of eyes that met his told the same message: *We stand with you.*

It gave him strength.

He squared his shoulders, opened the door, and stepped inside.

The taller agent, a broad man with a grim, set face stepped forward deliberately from his chair, spine ramrod straight.

"Mr. Watson," he said in a low, grave tone. "Special Agent Russell, DEA."

David extended his hand, calm and steady. "Special Agent Russell. Welcome to VirtuCare. How can I help you today?"

Russell didn't take the hand. His gaze was hard, accusing. "We are here under active federal investigation. The DEA has received evidence that VirtuCare is functioning as a platform for the illegal distribution of controlled substances. In short, Mr. Watson," his voice dropped lower "we believe this company is fueling the narcotics epidemic."

David's fingers curled loosely around the chair and sat. He looked each agent in the eyes, smiled and responded, "Oh, thank God."

"Excuse me?" Russel answered, somewhat taken aback.

"This company has never issued a prescription for a controlled substance. We are good on that front, sir."

"We have no intention of taking your word for it, Mr. Watson. My team is going to camp out in your offices until we look at every single file in every computer and file cabinet."

"Our doors are open to you and your team, Agent Russell. Whatever you ask for and need, my team will happily provide."

Russell was not accustomed to the quiet confidence exhibited by David Watson. He generally functioned in an atmosphere of fear and intimidation. "We will turn over every stone, and we will find the evidence."

"As I said, our doors are open, Agent Russell." David smiled. "Can I get anyone coffee, soda, or water?"

The investigation lasted three long months.

From the moment the DEA set up shop, their presence became a constant and heavy daily ordeal inside VirtuCare HQ.

Agents combed through every inch of the building. They hauled boxes of paper files out of storage. They scrutinized the EMR database down to the last keystroke.

The agents were never polite or nice. The VirtuCare team endured, and treated them with kindness and respect, never allowing the air of intimidation to adversely impact their day or their work.

Russell and his team traveled to San Antonio, rifling through records at the Physician Association HQ. Nothing was off limits: past, present, spoken, printed, or digital.

Every time Special Agent Russell himself came through the door, it was the same: a deep frown, curt orders, and the faint air of a man looking to catch someone, *anyone,* with their hand in the cookie jar.

He rarely spoke unless issuing commands. He never smiled, and he seemed to appear out of nowhere at the most inconvenient moments. Before long, VirtuCare's staff had adopted an unofficial nickname for him: "Mr. Grumpy."

It started as an innocent joke between two of the younger nurses. By week six, it had spread across the entire office. You could hear it in the hallway: *"Careful, Mr. Grumpy's in the small conference room,"* or, *"Mr. Grumpy is heading to IT! Good luck, guys."*

Doctor Burnes, who had a brother-in-law at the DEA, told everyone that they are trained to interact that way. He speculated that Grumpy was really a fun guy and a great family man.

No one bought in to that one.

Through the entire investigation, every file was spotless. Every EMR entry clean. Every flagged call traceable and properly documented.

In spite of all that, the strain was there, lingering just under the surface. Everyone knew it only took *one* mistake. If one doctor had felt sorry for a patient, and broken the rules, the whole company could go down.

David carried that weight most of all.

Day after day, as he walked the halls, he wondered: *Had they built a system capable of perfection on this front? What if they find something? And when the hammer drops… how do I protect this team?*

Three months to the day after the first raid, David arrived at HQ around 9:00 AM. He was running late from a breakfast meeting downtown.

The elevator dinged. As the doors opened, there he was, Special Agent Russell, AKA Mr. Grumpy, standing in the main hallway, arms folded, that same deep frown carved into his face.

Before David could speak, Russell barked: "Mr. Watson. In your office.

NOW."

David's pulse spiked.

This is it, he thought grimly. *They found something.*

A thousand possibilities rushed through his mind as he followed Russell down the hall. *Which doctor broke the protocol? Was it Rogers? Was it one of the new contractors? What system broke down so the prescription got through?*

By the time they reached his office, David was already preparing himself for the worst. He thought there would be court orders, licenses revoked, public headlines, the death of VirtuCare, and then prison. It was an ugly thought.

Russell stormed in first and dropped heavily into the chair across from David's desk. David sat opposite, calm but braced. "Alright, Agent Russell," he said quietly. "Tell me."

Russell's expression didn't change. He leaned forward, elbows on his knees, and then without preamble he said, "My team loves VirtuCare."

David blinked. "...Excuse me?"

Russell nodded, still scowling. "You heard me. We've been combing this company for three damn months. We have inspected every file and chart. We have looked at every call record, physician note, and prescription. My team has gone through more EMRs than I care to count." He paused. "And guess what we found?"

David swallowed. "What?"

"Nothing." Russell sat back. "Not a damn thing wrong. Not one illegal script. Not one misuse of controlled substances. Not one break in protocol. We have been as mean and intimidating as possible, and every single member of your team treated us with respect."

David exhaled slowly, the knot in his chest unwinding a fraction. "Well, that's good to hear."

Russell's frown deepened, though now David sensed it wasn't anger, just... the man's natural face. It wasn't a face he recognized.

"I'll tell you something else. Half of my agents have been traveling coast to coast for years. We get sick on the road, and you know what we didn't have? We never had good solution for healthcare. Until now, that is."

David stared, still trying to process what he was hearing.

Russell looked him dead in the eye. "VirtuCare works. It's fast. It's safe. Hell, it's better than half the care we've gotten through official channels."

David let out a breath, leaning forward on his desk. "Agent Russell... are you telling me the investigation is over?"

Russell nodded once. "Done. Closed. You're cleared."

David sat back, the full weight of the past three months lifting from his shoulders.

Then Russell added, almost gruffly: "And one more thing. We're putting VirtuCare on the approved vendor list for federal field agents.

Effective immediately."

David blinked again. "You're becoming... a customer?"

Russell grunted. "Damn right. When my people get sick in some hotel in Kansas or stuck on an op in Ohio, they'll be using VirtuCare. I've already cleared it with procurement. Just have your guy Gary Jefferson make the call."

For the first time, a smile tugged at the corner of David's mouth. "Well, Agent Russell, I can't say I expected that."

Russell stood, adjusting his jacket. "Don't thank me yet. I'm still Mr. Grumpy." He winked. "Yeah, I'm aware of the nickname, and it's fitting, even appropriate. Trust me, I have been called far worse."

And with that, he gave a curt nod and strode from the office, leaving David sitting alone, exhausted, relieved, and maybe, just maybe, a little amused.

* * *

It was Christmas Eve.

VirtuCare HQ had already emptied out. Even David had taken the evening off to spend time with Elaine. A few dozen physicians were working, but all were doing so from home, or some other holiday spot.

Snow flurries were drifting across Dallas—rare for Texas, but inside the system the virtual phones kept ringing. Patients didn't stop needing care over the holidays.

Dr. Mary Cohen was pulling holiday duty that night. She currently was licensed in 17 states, so for her it was a busy night. She was taking calls from her home office. Tree lights twinkling softly behind her, a four-month-old wedding ring on her finger, and most importantly, she was in her first trimester of her first pregnancy. Life was good.

Around 6:15 PM, a new consult hit her screen. She downloaded the medical record, reviewed, and called the west coast number.

"Hello, this is Doctor Mary Cohen from VirtuCare. How can I help you tonight, Mr. Jamison?"

The voice on the other end sounded strained and gravelly, breathless. "Doc... thank God... I need help. Seriously, thank God for VirtuCare. You guys are a life saver. I've run out of my oxy. My doctor's on vacation till after New Year's. I'm in agony."

Mary studied the patient profile *Paul Jameson.* New to the system. No prior encounters. No prior medical records on file.

She kept her tone calm, professional. "I'm sorry you're in pain, sir. But I want to be clear upfront, VirtuCare does not prescribe narcotics. We can recommend alternatives, but we do not issue oxycodone or similar medications through this service."

The voice cracked. "But, Doc... it's Christmas Eve. I'm hurtin bad. I got two kids here and they just want their daddy present for Christmas. I can't ruin it for them. I'm sure you understand that."

Mary's heart twinged, but her training held firm. "Sir, I'm very sorry. But this is a company-wide policy. We simply cannot and will not prescribe narcotics via telemedicine."

There was a beat of silence.

Then the voice grew desperate with low sobs leaking into the words. "Please... please... you don't know what it's like. I have good insurance, but no money to go to the pharmacy. The pain, it's so bad... Christmas is no time to be sufferin like this... I'm begging you, Doc."

Mary's hand tightened around her water glass. For a split second, she considered it. Jamison was right, Christmas with kids was no time to be in pain. Every instinct as a caregiver wanted to help, to fix it. But her training, her ethics, and her oath to the company held fast.

"I understand how difficult this must be," she said softly. "But again, narcotics are not an option through VirtuCare."

A wet, stuttering sob now. "Please... anything stronger... anything... just so I can get through tonight."

Mary took a slow breath.

"I can offer you a script for prescription-strength Ibuprofen. Your insurance will cover it if it's on a doctor's prescription." she said firmly. "It's effective for many types of pain and much safer in this situation. I can have our system send that to your pharmacy now."

The voice cracked again. "That's it? You won't even consider something stronger?"

Her tone stayed steady. "No, sir. Not through this service. I'm writing the Ibuprofen script now."

She finalized the note, signed off on the order, which pushed it to the

VirtuCare Nurse who would review the notes and call in the prescription to the pharmacy.

"I hope you feel better soon," she added softly, before ending the call.

She leaned back in her chair, exhaling slowly. That poor man. Her Christmas was officially ruined, now worrying about his wellbeing. Times like this made her want to just fly out to wherever he was, do an in-person consultation, and help him.

Still, even on Christmas Eve, *this* was why the protocols mattered. She had done the right thing.

* * *

Three hours after Mary Cohen issued the Ibuprofen prescription, the call recording landed in a secure folder on a private server in D.C. Ray Jamison sat in a small, dimly lit office, reporting to Crane's team via encrypted link.

On screen, Crane's face looked sour. Malor sat beside him, tapping an impatient finger on the desk.

"So... another failure," Crane muttered.

Jamison leaned toward the mic. "She held firm. Said no narcotics. Cried in front of her. I told her about my kids on Christmas. Cold hearted bitch just gave me Ibuprofen."

For a moment, Crane's jaw tightened in silent frustration.

Malor was reviewing the report and made a realization. "Wait... the call was placed from the western state residence we assigned, correct?"

Jamison nodded. "Yes. As instructed."

Malor glanced at Crane. "That state still has the five-day rule on any prescription issued over telemedicine or cross-coverage."

Crane's eyes lit with cold calculation. "Of course. She prescribed a ten-day course!"

Jamison shook his head. "Full prescription. I checked."

Crane smiled and felt the tingle of success. "Then we have them. We may not have caught her with opioids. But this... this is a technical violation of the state's telemedicine statute."

Malor's smile matched his. "And because that five-day limit is clearly on the books, it will hold in court. We won't even need to argue intent."

Crane's eyes gleamed now. "Prepare the summons, oh, and Jamison, you will need to stay in your role until this is over. It will give you another three of four months of pay.

* * *

Four days after Christmas, the process server arrived unannounced at VirtuCare HQ with an official summons addressed to both Dr. Mary Cohen and to VirtuCare, Inc.

David found Mary in her small office, reading patient notes. Her face paled slightly as he handed her the envelope.

"Looks like the first shot of the new year," David said grimly.

The summons cited violation of the five-day telemedicine prescription rule, scheduled for initial hearing in the western state's administrative court in late January.

David set his jaw. "We'll go together. No lawyers this time. Just the facts."

Mary nodded. "It was just Ibuprofen. I can't imagine they take that too seriously." Neither of them suspected that the "patient" was no patient at all.

The late January hearing took place in a small administrative courtroom two time zones west, the cold air biting and dry.

David and Mary sat alone at the front table since VirtuCare almost always chose not to bring lawyers, believing that lawyers would just escalate matters. If there was a possibility to negotiate, that was better done without legal teams. In their minds this would be little more than a minor regulatory session.

Board members questioned them under oath.

Mary spoke clearly and confidently, "We issued a prescription for prescription-strength Ibuprofen, appropriate for the presented symptoms. At no point did we issue controlled substances. The patient was warned multiple times of our policies."

David reinforced, "This was good medicine. There was no risk of harm to the patient."

Board member Suzanne Gonzalez asked why she even wrote a prescription when Ibuprofen could be purchased over the counter.

Doctor Cohen flipped through her notes, "The patient said he did not have money, but had good insurance. Even though I couldn't prescribe oxy, I was just trying to help."

"I see," Gonzalez responded. "Why did you prescribe for more than 5 days?"

"The patient told me his doctor would be gone until after New Years. Most prescriptions are ten days, and I felt it would amount to malpractice to write a term shorter than what would be required to resolve the patient's problem."

David added in calmly, "The statute forces physicians to write sub-standard courses of treatment. No physician should be compelled to issue half-treatments that violate clinical standards. This has been protested in multiple public forums."

The hearing ended quietly. No decision yet rendered.

By the time the second hearing convened in February, Mary was visibly in her second trimester, radiant, but clearly dealing with hormonal shifts that made the ordeal more emotionally charged.

Still, her testimony was clear and unwavering.

The Board pressed harder this time. Mary did not flinch.

As the hearing ended, it seemed that the Board had decided this was a case that was not worth pursuing. Doctor Cohen was a model citizen. She volunteered her time significantly more than most, served in the Reserves, and had no complaints anywhere on her record.

Mary and David still had no idea the "patient" had been planted. The actor's file remained sealed.

Doctor Gonzalez sent a recommendation to the Federal Board offices recommending the case be dropped. When Crane read the note, he was furious, responding that there would be a third hearing, and he would attend in person.

The third session began in mid-March. This time the Board room was full. Executive Director Crane was present.

Because of the somewhat unnecessary escalation, David broke his rule and brought in legal counsel, unaware of what awaited them.

Crane sat at the head of the table, his cold smile returning. He waited through formalities and introductions.

Then he spoke, his tone icy and deliberate:

"Dr. Cohen. Because of your violation of state statute, this Board intends to recommend permanent revocation of your license to practice medicine in this state. I am sure you are aware that ruling will domino to every state where you currently hold a license. Further, under provisions of federal statute, this case is being referred for criminal prosecution. I intend to recommend a prison term of no less than five years."

Gasps rippled through the few observers.

Mary paled visibly.

David's jaw tightened. "This has gone beyond anything reasonable,

Director Crane. Doctor Cohen is a patriot, a model citizen, and a beloved doctor. You are honestly saying she should serve a prison term?"

Crane stood, fists clenched. "Mr. Watson, this doctor is practicing a form of medicine that should not even be allowed in this country. It is not safe, and in our opinion, just a gimmick to enrich shareholders of VirtuCare. You should know that I do not intend to top prosecutions with this witch doctor you call a patriot. I intend to put you and your entire team behind bars and make a statement to the entire country that the Federal Board will not acquiesce to corporate greed."

"Prison?" One of the lawyers brought in by VirtuCare hissed under his breath. "For *Ibuprofen*? Has the Federal Board lost its collective mind?"

In spite of the fact that Gonzalez seemed to agree with VirtuCare, the hearing dragged on, with accusations mounting.

One of the lawyers for the Federal Board, reading from notes, stumbled slightly. "The actor... uhh, the patient's... the *individual posing as the patient*..." He stopped, flushing.

Silence filled the room. Everyone in the room was under oath.

David's eyes narrowed. "Actor?" he repeated, rising slowly from his seat. "Jamison is an *actor*?"

Crane glared at David, face tight. "It doesn't matter, Watson. Your witch doctor has broken the law."

David's voice rang through the chamber, steel-edged now. "No, Doctor

Crane, what you have done is called entrapment. You planted a false patient, scripted a scenario, and used that to generate a technical violation, so you could build this sham case."

Crane's voice came, cold as ice. "The Federal Board has its own processes, Mr. Watson. We have our courts, and our own judges. We are not subordinate to Federal Law. Our mandate is to protect the citizens of this country from the clear dangers posed by unchecked telemedicine."

David's eyes burned. "You're manufacturing crimes to justify your war on this company. You're breaking federal law."

The room was silent after David's outburst, with tension thick enough to cut.

At the Board's table, their lead counsel, a sharp-eyed attorney named Corbin, stood and cleared his throat.

"Given this new development regarding the actor patient," Corbin said carefully, "the Board's legal team requests a two-day recess to allow counsel for VirtuCare to process the discovery, and to ensure all procedural fairness."

There was no vote. The request was granted on the spot. The hearing adjourned.

David rose, helping Mary to her feet. Her hands were shaking. Tears welled in her eyes, not just from pregnancy hormones now, but from weeks of pressure finally breaking through.

"I thought I was going to lose everything," she whispered, voice trembling. "David, they plan to take my license and put me in prison for Ibuprofen."

David wrapped an arm around her shoulders and guided her quickly out of the courtroom. Behind them, the VirtuCare lawyers were gathering papers, already whispering among themselves.

Out in the cold hallway, Doctor Rogers, Byron, and Elaine were waiting.

David's face was carved in stone. His voice was low but burning. "This is criminal. They hired an effing actor to trick her, to entrap one of the finest doctors I know."

Mary wiped her face, still trembling. "And the Board, can they be charged for entrapment?"

One of the attorneys, a senior partner from VirtuCare's outside counsel, shook his head grimly. "It's a travesty, but the Federal Board operates under administrative authority. Entrapment law as applied in federal courts does not necessarily extend here. The Board can argue that their duty to investigate overrides entrapment defense. It's murky. I'll try to dig up case law, but... well, it doesn't look good."

David's jaw clenched. "They weaponized the system."

That night, back in his hotel, David barely slept.

The words echoed in his head. *Prison sentence... permanent license revocation... protect the citizens of this country from telemedicine...*

By 4:30 AM, he was up, pacing the room, running every angle.

Then, just after dawn, he made the call.

Laura Benjamin at CPR answered on the second ring.

"Laura, it's David."

"I got a little bit of the news," she said, voice alert despite the early hour. "Rough day yesterday."

"Worse," David replied. "I need the biggest hammer we can swing. We need this story national, today."

He laid out the whole thing, actor patient, false charges, Ibuprofen, federal overreach.

By the time he was done, Laura was already moving.

"Give me two hours," she said. "I know exactly who to call."

By noon, the story was everywhere.

**Federal Board Uses Actor to Entrap Young
Pregnant Doctor Over Ibuprofen Prescription**

**Telemedicine Giant Targeted
in Rogue Federal Investigation**

Doctor Mary Cohen Faces Prison for Prescribing Ibuprofen

The largest network in America ran it on the noon broadcast. Within an hour, other networks had picked it up. Simultaneously, social media exploded with #SaveDrCohen trending into the millions within hours.

Inside the Federal Board, the pressure to acquiesce mounted fast.

Crane's phone rang off the hook. Calls from political allies, from wary regulators, even calls from Senate staffers demanding answers.

By late afternoon, the damage was done.

Crane was forced to retreat.

The charges against Dr. Mary Cohen and VirtuCare were dropped and officially withdrawn from the docket. No prison sentence, no license revocation, no further charges.

Doctor Gonzalez called to apologize.

That night, back in Dallas, the VirtuCare team gathered at HQ. The relief was palpable, but the victory bittersweet.

David stood in the middle of the conference room, voice low but steady. "The good news is that Mary is clear. This chapter is officially over." A ripple of applause, hugs, and tears followed.

"But," he added, voice tightening, "make no mistake, this was a skirmish win in a much bigger war. My intelligence at the Federal Board is telling me they will blame this on Professor Malor, Crane will go unscathed, and the Board is now tipped against us. Bottom line, this wasn't a win. Not really. We embarrassed them. And now the Federal Board is against us... probably openly. They won't stop, and the next shot... will be harder."

The room was quiet.

Everyone knew it was true.

The phalanx had held the line, but the war was still far from over.

* * *

David rarely asked for advice. But after the relentless fight with the

Federal Board, after watching Mary break down in that courtroom, and after three months of walking the razor's edge, he knew it was time.

There was only one man to call.

Nathan Martin was an old friend, a mentor, and one of VirtuCare's first true believers.

Years ago, when VirtuCare was just a fragile startup with a risky future, Nathan had told David: *"You're going to change medicine. This will become a multi-billion-dollar industry, and you're the right man to be at the front of it. Not by yourself, of course. The vision of Byron Cook and all the people you bring to the table will be critical to making that happen, but David, it will happen."*

Nathan had been right, and he'd always been there when David needed a sounding board.

David placed the call to his dear friend on a quiet Wednesday morning, who answered on the second ring. His familiar voice warm, but a little thinner than usual.

"David Watson. I was wondering when you'd call."

David smiled. "I could use your wisdom."

Nathan chuckled. "I'm in Europe right now. Long trip, but I'm back in Texas on Saturday. Coffee?"

"Perfect."

That Saturday morning, they met at their old spot—an unassuming coffee shop in Frisco Texas, near the Stonebriar Mall.

When David walked in, Nathan rose to greet him, warm, slightly balding, and sharp-eyed as ever. David noticed it at once: something in the man's face, a slight pallor, a thinner frame.

They hugged.

"You look tired," David said quietly.

Nathan waved it off. "Just running too fast. You know how it is."

David didn't push. Not yet.

They settled into their corner booth. Over strong black coffee, David poured out the whole story with Crane, the Federal Board, the entrapment, the public fight, the win, and the deepening war ahead.

Nathan listened without interrupting, his sharp mind tracking every move.

When David finished, Nathan sat back, fingers steepled.

"You've crossed the line now, David," he said quietly. "They won't stop. You embarrassed them publicly so you can 100% guarantee they'll come at you again. This time even harder."

David nodded grimly, "I know."

Nathan's eyes gleamed. "Then you need to move faster than they can. Change the battlefield."

"How?"

Nathan smiled faintly. "Two things."

He leaned forward.

"First, call my friend Pam Bond. She's a young attorney in Florida. She's smart as hell, ambitious, and quite capable of drafting legislation. She's already drafted several state-level health bills. I guarantee, if you ask her, she'll help you write the first piece of real telemedicine legislation in this country. It'll be good for her career and should become something that can start turning the tide with."

David's eyes lit. "You think she'd do it?"

Nathan grinned. "I *know* she will. Of course, I'll call her after our meeting and put the bug in her ear."

"I'll do it, Nathan. What's the second thing?"

Nathan gave a sly look. "Second, I know you're smart enough, so you're seeing that firecracker Elaine, aren't you?"

David laughed. "You know me too well."

Nathan's grin widened. "Pop the question."

David blinked.

Nathan went on. "David, women like her? They don't come around twice in life. You've built a company, fought for an industry, protected your people... don't forget to build a life, too. It's time. Tie that knot."

David felt something warm settle in his chest. He gave a quiet nod. "I'll think about it."

Nathan slapped his arm. "Don't think too long."

Four days later, the call came.

Nathan's wife, voice shaking, told David that Nathan had died. It was sepsis from an infection he'd picked up overseas.

David sat in his office after the call, stunned. A hollow ache spreading through him.

Gone. Just like that.

But Nathan's words lived on.

Over the next few weeks, David threw himself into the work. He called Pam Bond. They connected immediately. Nathan was right, she was fierce, brilliant, and fast-moving. Most importantly, she was enough to make David get over his general aversion to lawyers. Together they drafted the first comprehensive telemedicine legislation in U.S. history. The bill was strong enough to pave the way forward, and to protect companies like VirtuCare from these outdated assaults.

Three months later... the law passed. A milestone for the industry.

And for David, with the settling tide, now was the time to keep the second promise to his old friend. It was one that had been carefully considered, and Nathan had been right. Elaine *was* once in a lifetime.

A few days after the legislation passed, David asked Elaine to take a weekend trip.

"Where to?" she asked, eyes sparkling.

"Guadalupe."

The trail was as they remembered: rocky, steep, and winding through the high desert pines. The cool wind swept across the peaks as they climbed, boots crunching on stone, hearts beating in sync.

Near the summit, they stopped—catching their breath and taking in the endless view of West Texas sprawling below.

Once on the summit, David turned toward her, heart thudding.

"You know," he said softly, "last time we were here... I realized something."

Elaine smiled, brushing wind-blown hair from her face. "What's that?"

David reached into his pack and pulled out a small velvet box.

"That I never want to climb another mountain, literal or otherwise, without you."

Elaine's eyes widened, her breath catching.

David opened the box. A simple, elegant ring catching the sunlight.

"Elaine Singer," he said, voice steady, full of warmth. "Will you marry me?"

For a heartbeat, there was only the wind, then, tears brimming, Elaine laughed through a radiant smile.

"Yes. Yes, David. Of course, yes."

He slipped the ring onto her finger, drawing her close. They kissed beneath the wide Texas sky, two hearts, stronger together than either had ever been alone.

And as they stood on that mountain, in the place where it all began... they knew the hardest fights were still ahead.

But now, they would face them together.

10

Telemedicine Lawfare

Benedict Crane sat alone at the long walnut conference table in the Board's D.C. headquarters, the morning sun glinting harshly through the tall windows. Professor Malor was gone, having dutifully accepted his role as scapegoat after the actor-patient debacle. Crane felt neither relief nor regret. Malor had served his purpose, and would be sorely missed, but he had accepted his departure as part of the larger goal of protecting healthcare from telemedicine.

Now the mission belonged to Crane alone.

Three of the more loyal Board members filed into the room: Dr. Janice Ferrell from Illinois, Dr. Marcus Hsu from California, and attorney Robert Sloan, a ruthless litigator known for creative interpretations of healthcare statutes. They nodded at Crane, their faces set. They were true believers in the mission: stop telemedicine and companies like VirtuCare at any cost.

Crane wasted no time. "VirtuCare and the entire telemedicine industry continues to grow. More states, more patients, more press. This is dangerous." His voice was clipped, controlled.

Dr. Hsu tapped a manila file. "Their outcomes are good. Hard to fight on quality or patient safety."

"True," Crane admitted. "But that's not where we'll hit them."

Attorney Sloan opened his laptop. "We've done a deep dive into their public communications, website, emails, thought leadership articles, and public speeches. They're skirting the edges of state advertising laws."

Crane's eyes sharpened. "Go on."

"In at least twenty states, doctors are prohibited from *advertising* clinical services. What VirtuCare calls 'information' crosses that line in several jurisdictions. They make promises about fast diagnoses and simplified care. It's textbook violation."

A slow smile crept across Crane's face. "That's a good start. Are we singularly focused on VirtuCare?"

"I think our resources are best spent with focus, so yes," Sloan answered. "Once we take down VirtuCare, the industry will follow."

The Board members leaned in as Sloan outlined the plan: "Use existing state statutes to trigger enforcement actions. Target advertising violations as an entry point. The internet is everywhere, technically in all 50 states, so we should have good Interstate Commerce Clause cases to support us. We can use those violations to demand license reviews and, where possible, shutdown orders. If VirtuCare is crippled in enough states, it will wither before the courts or public opinion can save it."

The Board voted unanimously to proceed.

News of the Board's maneuver reached David Watson within days. He called an emergency meeting with Byron Cook and the VirtuCare legal team. For the first time in the company's history, Watson felt the full weight of the Board's wrath.

"This isn't some regulatory letter," Byron said, scanning the documents. "They're going for the jugular."

"We need a top-tier firm," David replied. "No offense to our counsel, but this is national warfare. Let's hire the best of the best."

Within a week, VirtuCare retained one of the most powerful law firms in the country. Their lead attorney, Deborah Lennox, came highly recommended. She was a litigator who had gone toe-to-toe with government agencies, and had always won.

Lennox stood in the war room at VirtuCare's HQ, flipping through the Board's filings. "They think they've got us boxed in," she said coolly. "But they've underestimated us."

Her team filed for an emergency injunction arguing that VirtuCare's communications were lawful, protected speech, and that the Board's actions would cause irreparable harm to patients, payors, and corporations relying on VirtuCare services.

Three weeks later, history was made.

For the first time in U.S. medical history, a federal judge granted an injunction *against* the Board, preventing them from shutting down VirtuCare while the legal battle unfolded.

David stood outside the courtroom, a mix of relief and grim resolve. "We bought time. Now we fight."

And fight, they did.

Over the next three years, lawsuits and countersuits ricocheted through courthouses in Texas, Florida, New York, and California. The company was forced to become a legal machine with injunctions, appeals, partial victories, and temporary defeats.

The battle consumed millions in legal fees, and constantly garnered the attention of the entire healthcare industry. It became the Superbowl of healthcare. No one had ever challenged the Boards at this level. No one had ever dared.

In one hearing, a judge leaned over the bench and remarked, "VirtuCare isn't just fighting for itself. You're setting the precedent for the future of medicine."

David walked out of that hearing knowing one thing: If they lost, it was over, not just for VirtuCare, but for telemedicine itself.

In the time they fought those battles, David would be named Ernst & Young Entrepreneur of the Year, and the Company would be named by MIT as one of the 50 smartest companies in the World. Patient population grew into the tens of millions, while holding customer satisfaction ratings 30 points above all other sectors, fulfilling Klark Thomas' long dream of telemedicine becoming part of the mainstream. In spite of all those accolades, some states still opposed telemedicine care for their residents.

Despite of all the wins, the Federal Board was slowly chipping away at the fortification VirtuCare had built. Most analysts posited that the Board would ultimately prevail were it not for a spring day in D.C., weeks away from what should have been the final hearing.

* * *

Benedict Crane speared a piece of grilled salmon and glanced over the rim of his wine glass at his old friend, Susan Hatchfield, seated across from him.

They were in a dim corner of *Le Pavillon du Midi*, one of D.C.'s quieter bistros, a favorite for lobbyists, regulators, and old-line federal staffers who preferred their scheming with a side of elegance. It was mid-week, the place half full, with the hum of discreet conversation serving as the perfect camouflage.

Susan was currently serving in a mid-level director slot at HHS and was known for her knack for staying out of trouble. She swirled her Bordeaux and leaned in. "You've been at this for years now, Benedict. Honestly, I cannot figure out why this fight is so important to you? You are winning the war, but the evidence is leaning their way. Telemedicine's been around for a while now and it's clearly not dangerous. Hell, most of the hospitals are using some version of it now."

Crane's jaw tightened for a beat before he exhaled slowly. "You're not wrong, Susan. Telemedicine has proven useful, especially for rural gaps and chronic care management. In some ways, I will admit, it's a legitimate tool…"

Susan smiled faintly, thinking perhaps the conversation was turning toward reason.

But then Crane's tone shifted to harder, lower tones, and his eyes turned cold. "But VirtuCare? That's something else entirely. Watson and Klark are smug bastards. And that pack of doctors parading as innovators, pushing their for-profit circus into an industry that should be governed by discipline, by the sacred trust of medicine? They broke the old order. They humiliated our Board, and they embarrassed me."

Susan arched a brow. "So… this *is* personal?"

Crane leaned closer, voice sharp now. "Damn right it's personal. They've turned medicine into a tech startup game, hawking convenience over quality. And now they've built an empire off of what used to be a disciplined calling. I won't rest until VirtuCare is shut down. Completely shut down and out of business. Susan, if I had my way," he set down his fork with a quiet finality, "every one of those bastards who call themselves executives would be behind bars. Watson. Cook. Klark. All of them."

Susan blinked, slightly taken aback. "That sounds a bit extreme. Rationally, Benedict, is this really worth that kind of vendetta?" She began to not recognize the ruthless rage painted all over her old friend's face.

Crane's expression hardened, he seethed. "I never said it's rational, at least, not in the last couple years. It's *not* rational. But it is what I want. It's my goal, Susan. They hurt me and my mentor, Victor Malor, and I've come *too* far to let this go now."

Neither Crane nor Susan noticed the woman seated alone at the next table, a thin spiral notebook resting next to her glass of iced tea. Sarah Welles, a staff reporter for the *Washington Post*, had stopped mid-bite when she heard *"VirtuCare"* and *"behind bars"* in the same sentence. For the last ten minutes, her recorder ran and her pen moved quietly, steadily, capturing every word.

The following morning, Watson's phone buzzed at 6:15 AM with an alert from Laura, the CEO of VirtuCare's PR firm.

The headline wasn't front page, but it was on page 2 of the *Post*:

Federal Board Leader Vows to 'Destroy' Telemedicine Pioneer

The pull quote, which was boxed in bold:

I agree it's not rational. But destroying VirtuCare is my goal.

David Watson stared at the screen, lips curling into a wry, humorless smile. *"Well, Benedict,"* he muttered while dialing Byron, *"looks like you just handed us the final victory in this war."*

* * *

Whitin hours of the news article's publication, the Federal Board of Medical Examiners met in an emergency closed session. The corridors of the building were quiet, but inside the boardroom, the atmosphere was tense. Benedict Crane sat stiffly at the long oak table, eyes locked on the chairman, Dr. Samuel Klein.

Klein cleared his throat. "Doctor Crane, after careful review of a long string of events, including this morning's unfortunate appearance in the *Post,* the Board has determined that your continued presence is no longer in the best interests of this organization or its mission. Over the years of your directorship the national opinion and acceptance of telemedicine has grown. We recognize that even you have come to accept telemedicine, at least to some degree. The problem stems from the fact that this organization cannot be used as a tool for executing vendettas."

Crane's jaw tightened. He opened his mouth to object, but Klein raised a hand.

"This is not a debate," Klein continued. "You are hereby dismissed, effective immediately. Security will escort you to collect your personal items."

The words hit Crane like a hammer. The room began to blur. Fired. After all his years of accomplishments, and all of his battles.

Two days later, Crane sat in a sleek office at the headquarters of United TeleCare Systems, a rising competitor in the telemedicine industry. The CEO had reached out within hours of the *Post* article, "You know the field better than anyone," the man had said. "We'd be fools not to bring you in."

Benedict Crane, former arch-critic of telemedicine, signed a contract as United's new Chief Medical Officer. Hs salary tripled from the pay scale he had been earning in the Federal Board, and he took a nice block of stock options while he was at it.

Later that week, Klark and David met for dinner at their favorite Italian restaurant in Addison. They clinked glasses of Chianti and dug into steaming plates of pasta.

"You hear the news?" Klark asked with a sly smile.

David wiped his mouth with a napkin. "About Crane?"

"Yep. Chief Medical Officer. United TeleCare."

David laughed out loud. "You're kidding."

"Nope. Even the great Benedict Crane can't fight the tide of telemedicine forever!"

David shook his head, grinning. "Our tidal wave must be bigger than I thought, to have swept in a naysayer like him."

Klark leaned back, eyes twinkling. "One by one, my friend. They all come around."

David raised his glass again. "Think about the battles we have fought, Klark. The world is changing, and we have finally made it to the eye of the storm." David paused, then raised his glass. "Here's to Doctor Klark Thomas, The Father of Telemedicine."

Klark nearly choked on his wine. "Oh, come on, David. If anyone deserves that title, it's Larry Charles. He was talking about this stuff before most of us even knew what a modem was."

David shook his head, remaining on point. "Larry was the visionary, sure, but you, my friend, you're the one who spent years in the trenches. You planted the seeds, built the networks, fought the battles. You never gave up and you're the reason telemedicine is mainstream now."

Klark chuckled. "Like I said, you're giving me too much credit, David."

"I'm not, and tonight, I'm putting it on the record."

They laughed, sparring playfully for a few moments more. Then Klark leaned in, eyes warm with pride. "Well, if I am the father," he said, raising his glass again, "then you and Byron are my sons. And I couldn't be prouder of the men you've become."

David clinked his glass once more, his smile broad. The future was coming fast, and they were ready for it together.

11

Perfect Vision

The conference room was nearly empty—most of the VirtuCare team was dialed in on screens. It was late March 2020, and the pandemic was rewriting every playbook in healthcare.

David stood at the head of the table, laptop open, video feeds glowing across the wall. In the years since he had first taken the CEO slot, technology, video conferencing, and remote medicine had risen up to meet most challenges.

Today, the entire team was on a video conference using Zoom, a tool everyone at VirtuCare knew how to use, and one the world would soon embrace.

"All right, team," he began. His voice was steady, but his expression was tight. "Here's where we are today."

He clicked a slide forward.

"Worldwide cases: 500,000 confirmed. Deaths: over 23,000. The U.S. alone crossed 85,000 cases this morning. Every day, these numbers grow. Hospitals are overrun. ERs are at capacity in New York, Seattle, and Chicago."

The screen went black for a beat as he looked out at the VirtuCare team through a camera small enough to fit in the palm of his hand.

"You know… back in January, we were joking that 2020 was going to be *the year of perfect vision,*" he said, half smiling. "That clever 20/20 marketing pitch. A year of clarity, new horizons. Optimism was everywhere, and, well," he glanced at the statistics on the screen, "we've got new horizons, just not the ones we expected."

The room was quiet.

"We are the entrepreneurs, the innovators, and the tomorrow-makers. My friends, this is what we built for," David continued, his voice rising with conviction. "For years we've faced down critics, regulators, and skeptics. Now the entire healthcare system is going to need telemedicine…because there's no other choice. We *are* the front line now."

Byron, Klark, and Jennice, along with dozens of staffers and faces on the screen, nodded back.

"This nation is going to need us to remain calm, like we did the day the DEA came to our office with their guns and badges," David took a breath, reached into his folder. "Before we close," he said, "I want to read something."

He unfolded a crisp sheet of stationery, the signature of a former U.S. Surgeon General embossed at the top.

"This letter came this morning," David held up the document so everyone on video could see. "It's a letter form a former US Surgeon General, someone who watched as we fought so many battles to get to where we are today."

He began to read:

> *To David, Byron, Klark, and the entire VirtuCare team,*
>
> *For many years, I watched your struggle. I saw how hard you fought to build what so many said could not be done. You persisted when most would have walked away and pushed telemedicine into the mainstream. Your efforts gave it credibility, scale, and trust.*
>
> *Now, as our nation faces this historic pandemic, it is clear: without the engine you built, our healthcare system would be on the verge of collapse. Because of VirtuCare and companies like it, countless lives will be saved. Your work has become a critical part of our national response.*
>
> *On behalf of the public health community, and from me personally, thank you. Stay strong. Keep leading.*
>
> *-KSM, Former U.S. Surgeon General*

David looked up from the letter, eyes a little glassy. The team on-screen was silent for a moment, then a few began clapping. The sound grew.

"This is our moment," David said quietly. "Let's rise to it."

* * *

VirtuCare's servers hummed around the clock. Demand was spiking at a rate none of them could have predicted.

In the early days of the pandemic, the company's entire physician network focused almost exclusively on COVID-related cases, with patients too afraid or unable to go to a hospital, desperate for answers about symptoms, exposure, and treatment.

The company's average daily visit volume, once in the tens of thousands, tripled, then quadrupled. The engine built by Michelle with later revisions and updates from Noel who bult version 2, then Jeff who built all later versions, stood solid through the years and all the growth.

Jennice Walters ran triage from her home office, hair pulled back, eyes sharp behind her glasses, her daughter, Mary, often did more consults than she did, in spite of her three children at home.

VirtuCare doctors were fielding fevers, shortness of breath, and lost sense of taste and smell. Mostly, the VirtuCare doctors were a calm voice in the storm, an expert who could use the magic of telemedicine to come into the patient's home in a scary, uncertain time.

Doctors logged on from everywhere: retired clinicians reactivated, part-timers moved to full shifts. Virtual training sessions taught them the latest CDC guidance as it evolved, sometimes by the hour.

One day in early April, Byron hopped on a call with the CEO of a regional hospital system in Michigan. Their emergency rooms were collapsing under the weight of COVID cases.

"We can't handle this surge," the CEO admitted. "Can you help?"

Within 24 hours, VirtuCare had spun up a custom telemedicine portal for the hospital, allowing their own doctors to screen and manage non-urgent patients virtually, keeping thousands of people out of waiting rooms where they might contract or spread the virus.

"Your portal saved us," the Michigan CEO later wrote to Byron. "Without it, we would've been sunk."

Klark, watching all of this unfold, couldn't help but marvel at how far they'd come.

"We're not just treating VirtuCare patients anymore," he told David over Zoom. "We're giving the whole country an engine. A model."

He was right. Requests poured in from small clinics, hospital networks, government agencies, and even big employers who wanted VirtuCare's playbook to protect their workforces.

And the public was noticing too.

News anchors began calling it the "telemedicine revolution." Major papers ran stories with headlines like: *Telehealth Steps in Where Hospitals Can't.*

In late April, a CNN reporter asked David in a live interview: "Did you ever imagine telemedicine would become this critical, this fast?"

David answered with a tired smile: "We hoped it would. We just didn't expect it to happen under these circumstances."

Behind the scenes, every VirtuCare team member was pulling 14-hour days. Techs scaled the cloud infrastructure to keep up with soaring demand. Doctors treated patients between caring for their own families in lockdown.

And in those long, intense weeks, something shifted, for the public, for regulators, and even for the skeptics.

Telemedicine wasn't the future anymore. It was the present.

* * *

It was late July, and the Texas heat shimmered outside the window when Elaine's phone rang.

She smiled when she saw the caller ID: her sister, Shirley.

"Hey you," Elaine answered, settling into her office nook with a glass of iced tea. "What's up?"

Shirley's voice was half laughing already. "You are not going to believe the call I just got."

"Try me."

"My doctor's office called to check in, you know, routine stuff, but then the nurse asks me… would I be okay seeing the doctor over… wait for it… this new thing called *telemedicine*."

Elaine burst out laughing. "Oh no! Not the dreaded newfangled telemedicine! Did anyone die?"

"That's what I said! I told her, 'Honey, my sister's been living and breathing that stuff for years. Y'all are just figuring this out now?'"

They both giggled.

"Seriously though," Shirley went on, "they acted like it was some space-age breakthrough."

"Well," Elaine said, wiping tears of laughter from her eyes, "considering how hard David, Klark, and Byron fought to drag healthcare into the 21st century, I guess it *is* a breakthrough—for them."

"Looks like you're all finally winning," Maggie said warmly. "It's about time."

Elaine smiled. "Feels like it."

David Watson thought about the last couple years in healthcare as he stood at the front of the glass-walled room, sleeves rolled, a pot of coffee half gone on the side table. Around him were Byron, Klark, Jennice, Mary, Corey, and Elaine, who was both his wife and now COO of the company. There were several newer executives who had joined as VirtuCare scaled to a national presence, including a CTO named Jeff and a Chief Marketing Officer named Orin. The newcomers would never know the challenges of the early days and would have to stop themselves from yawning when the original executives reminisced. Those battles seemed surreal and existed only in the minds of the founders. The company now faced new challenges that consumed time and energy.

The pandemic had changed *everything.*

David clicked to a slide:

COVID-19: U.S. Impact on Healthcare Utilization

"Before COVID," he began, "telemedicine made up less than 1% of outpatient visits nationally."

He flipped to the next slide:

- **April 2020: 46% of Americans used telemedicine for at least one encounter.**
- **2021: 24% of *all* outpatient care was delivered virtually.**
- **2022: 71% of patients preferred telemedicine over in-person for routine issues.**
- **2023: 85% of patients preferred telemedicine over in-person.**
- **Satisfaction ratings remain at 94-96%.**

David paused. "You know... people used to say 2020 would be the year of perfect vision," he said wryly. "And in a way, it was. The pandemic forced healthcare, the States, the Federal Board, and patients to see what was possible when old barriers came down."

Byron nodded. "What took us two decades to fight for happened in six months."

David smiled. "And VirtuCare went from 500,000 encounters a year to 6 million. All in the course of two years."

The group let that sink in.

Corey Rogers leaned back in his chair, arms crossed. "Hard to believe, after everything. I still remember being grilled in front of Crane. Now half my classmates from med school are asking how to get in on this."

Mary Cohen laughed. "Heck, my old residency program just launched a 'virtual care' fellowship. They say it's the next frontier."

Klark grinned. "Funny how all the 'voodoo medicine' is now core curriculum."

"Hah," Mary laughed. "The board called me a witch doctor. I should get a plaque for that one!"

Jennice added softly, "It's because it works. And because people needed it to work."

David nodded. "Exactly. The data backs it up. Lower ER visits. Higher adherence to treatment. Faster access to care. Fewer unnecessary antibiotics. And patient satisfaction? Still the highest in healthcare."

"Okay, okay," Jeff started, "let's get past all this and focus on the current challenges."

David studied Jeff. Maybe it was time to do another Guadalupe trip and see if he could still keep up with Elaine the mountain goat.

"A little patience, Jeff. I want us to take a moment to reflect on what we've done. Not just what we survived, but what we built. This was never about the tech. It was about creating a version of care that focused on what matter–the doctors and the patients. When the world needed it most, we were ready, but to your point, the real question for the innovators is, what is next?"

Byron raised a coffee cup and jokingly frowned at Jeff and Orin. "To the team that made it happen."

They all raised glasses, mugs, water bottles

David's eyes twinkled. "And to the future. Because this is just the beginning.”

Klark leaned in. “You know, when Larry Charles and I first tinkered with those old TVs back at Logan, we never imagined this. Not in our wildest dreams.”

David smiled. “And yet, here we are.”

Jennice tilted her head playfully. “Klark, if you’re the father of telemedicine, I guess that makes the rest of us your unruly children.”

“Unruly is a good name for the lot of you,” Klark answered, “but I’m getting a bit old to play the role of father.

David laughed. “Well, if Klark’s the father, then Byron was the idea man who brought the revolution home.”

Klark chuckled. “Okay children, I’d say we’re one hell of a family. Now let’s all get back to work. It seems our non-children guests are tired of our constant bragging about the past.”

They all laughed, the mood warm but proud.

Across the room, Elaine caught David’s eye. “We’re not done yet. The next frontier is making sure this isn’t just a pandemic bump. It’s the new normal. Technology is accelerating every day. Most companies can’t keep up with the pace.”

David nodded. “Right. We’ve proven it works. Now we have to make sure it stays accessible and affordable, everywhere.”

He clicked to one final slide, it was a quote from Larry Charles, unearthed from an old interview:

"Telemedicine isn't about replacing doctors. It's about making doctors available to more people, more often, more humanely."

David closed the laptop.

"No better words to end on," he said.

The room was quiet, reflective, each person thinking about the journey and the long road from resistance to revolution.

But the Revolution was now over…

* * *

David glanced at his calendar mid-morning and paused at an entry he'd nearly forgotten:

Lunch with Mary Cohen (Conf Room).

He smiled. Mary had been one of VirtuCare's earliest and longest standing physicians and was clearly famous for having survived the turbulent Ibuprofen case eighteen years earlier. She'd stuck with the company through every high and low.

What surprised him more was the note in parentheses: "+ Corey."

At noon, the conference room door opened and in stepped Mary, still trim and confident in her signature jeans and smock. Beside her stood a tall, young man with tousled dark hair, piercing eyes, and an unmistakable aura of curiosity. He looked just like Corey Rogers.

"David," Mary said, her smile warm. "I hope you don't mind; I brought my eldest. He's been begging to meet you."

David stood and extended his hand. "Of course not. You must be

Corey. This company would not have been possible without the support of your mom and dad."

Corey grinned and shook his hand firmly. "It's an honor, sir. I've heard about VirtuCare since... well, pretty much my whole life. My mom used to tell me stories when I was little about when she was pregnant with me, fighting the Ibuprofen case." He laughed.

David chuckled. "You were part of this company before you were even born, then. Welcome back. Have you ever thought about the fact that you could have been born in prison?" He joked.

"I have, and you're right, it is quite the story and legacy."

David gestured to the table where lunch was set up. "Come, grab some food and tell me what you're up to these days."

They casually sat and relaxed. Corey wasted no time. "I've been diving deep into AI models, natural language processing, and large-scale operating systems. Healthcare is such a mess when it comes to tech integration. From what I can see, it feels like every EMR is a Frankenstein of outdated code. I've been thinking about ways AI could streamline diagnostics and even patient flow, especially for remote care."

David raised an eyebrow, impressed. "Wow, that's quite the bundle of analysis. You sound like someone I should be hiring."

Corey laughed. "Maybe one day, sir. For now, I'm just trying to learn as much as I can. Actually... I *was* wondering..." He hesitated, glanced at his mom, then pushed forward. "Would you ever consider introducing me to Noel Gern, Dr. Castro, and Michelle Bianchi? I've followed their work, especially Castro's recent papers on predictive analytics for remote triage. I'd love the chance to talk with them... even if it's just to ask a few questions."

David leaned back, smiling. The young man's enthusiasm was infectious. "I think they'd like that. In fact, I'll set it up myself." He glanced at Mary. "You've raised a sharp one, Mary."

Mary beamed, pride unmistakable. "He keeps Corey and me on our toes, but with two MDs for parents, I cannot figure out where the love of computers and data came from."

David looked back to Corey. "How about this, we're hosting a tech roundtable next month. I'll make sure you're invited. In the meantime, I'll ping Noel, Paul, and Michelle. If we can get them here, I'm sure they'd be happy to meet a future innovator."

Corey's grin widened. "That would be amazing. Thank you, sir. Really."

"Well, Noel is working at another company, and Michelle is now a stay-at-home mom training dogs, but I am sure both of them would love to chat and meet you. I haven't spoken with Castro in some time, but you're right, he's on the cutting edge."

David raised his glass of iced tea. "To the next generation."

They clinked glasses, and in that small, unassuming moment, the seed of another chapter in VirtuCare's story was quietly planted.

Epilogue
The Seeds of a new Future

Late April 2024

David had just wrapped a long day of board meetings when his phone buzzed with a text from Paul Castro:

"Time for a quick meeting? Corey and I have something big."

Intrigued, David texted back:

"Come to my office."

Fifteen minutes later, Paul and Corey walked in, both visibly energized, carrying a laptop and a thick folder of notes.

David motioned them to sit. "Okay. You've got my attention."

Paul opened the laptop, turning the screen toward David. "We've been building this for three months now. It's an AI diagnostic engine that runs parallel to the VirtuCare EMR. It analyzes patient records, medical history, symptoms, vitals, and captures data from anything the patient has, like smart watches, bathroom scales, and, well, pretty much everything. You currently have medical records for 100 million patients. Think about it. No one had more EMR than VirtuCare."

"What's the objective, Paul?"

"It uses AI to catch and flag problems, long before most patients even know they have one. It also assists doctors quietly in the background to suggest possible diagnoses and identify patterns doctors might miss."

Corey chimed in, eyes bright. "It also learns over time. The more cases it sees, the more refined it becomes. Eventually, it could reduce diagnostic errors by orders of magnitude."

David leaned in. "What kind of errors are we talking about?"

Paul didn't hesitate. "Johns Hopkins did a study last year. They reported that over 250,000 patients die annually in the U.S. from medical errors, most of them diagnostic. It's the third leading cause of death, David. This engine could change that."

"Holy crap," David started incredulously. "You're telling me that there are 250,000 deaths in this country, annually, from medical mistakes?"

"That's what the Hopkins study reported."

David sat back, considering the scope of what they were proposing.

Paul continued, "We want to form a new AI division inside VirtuCare. It would operate as a core component of your EMR. Every doctor on the platform would have access. Every patient would benefit."

For a long moment, David said nothing, fingers steepled beneath his chin. Finally, he asked, "What's the catch?"

Paul exchanged a glance with Corey. "It'll be very controversial."

"Why?" David asked.

"Because it changes the role of the physician," Paul said calmly. "It puts AI in a position to flag things doctors miss. It forces transparency. The Federal Board of Medical Examiners probably won't like it."

"They'll probably bring Crane back in for this one," David joked.

"I don't know, but many traditional providers will hate it. They'll say it undermines clinical judgment and threatens their autonomy."

David let out a long breath. "All the usual suspects, and you're probably right."

He looked at the two men. Paul was the seasoned informatics pioneer, and Corey, full of energy and great ideas, was the brilliant new mind just beginning his journey and continuing his mom and dad's fight.

"You understand that this is a line in the sand, and the beginning of a new war?"

"Yes, sir."

David took a deep breath and smiled faintly.

"Let's do it."

Please go to Amazon,
and write a review for this book!

-Thank you,
Michael, Jay, and Harvey.

Author Biographies

Michael Gorton, BSEE, MS Physics, Juris Doctorate, is a serial entrepreneur who has founded 15 companies, including Teladoc, the world's largest telemedicine company. A winner of the prestigious Ernst & Young Entrepreneur of the Year Award, and known for work in telemedicine, AI, and business strategy. Gorton is also a natural born storyteller, an accomplished author, and a keynote speaker. Along with Teladoc, Gorton's companies include Internet Global, Palo Duro Records, Texas Acceleration Group. Principal Solar and Recuro Health.

Gorton's books are grounded in the breakthroughs of tomorrow, filled with adventure, science, romance and ultimate questions about humanity and the universe. He has written 6 #1 bestsellers and won over a dozen awards for his books which include both fiction and nonfiction. His previous books, including Broken Handoff (named the #1 M&A book by Book Authority) and Calamistunity: The Secret to Success, have cemented his reputation as an expert in leadership and innovation. Digital Medical Home tells the history of telemedicine from its introduction in the 1960s to modern times. His fiction, including the historical novel Forefathers & Founders, won several awards, reached #1 and has resonated with readers. Tachyon Tunnel received critical acclaim for its thought-provoking take on time travel, and innovative use of tachyons for interstellar travel. Tachyon Tunnel 2 stayed on the bestseller list for over a month and received 6 coveted awards for fiction.

Jay H. Sanders, M.D., FACP, FACAAI, FATA is a consultant on this book and widely recognized as the "Father of Telemedicine." He is CEO of The Global Telemedicine Group and Professor of Medicine (Adjunct) at Johns Hopkins University. Dr. Sanders founded the first statewide telemedicine system and pioneered innovations like tele-homecare and correctional telemedicine. He served as the sole civilian on the DOD Telemedicine Board and has advised NASA, the FCC, WHO, and numerous global institutions. He earned his M.D. magna cum laude from Harvard and completed his residency at Massachusetts General Hospital.

He helped to form the American Telemedicine Association (ATA), and orchestrated Bernard Harris, MD giving a keynote for the ATA while Doctor Harris was an astronaut. That speech was given from Space!

Doctor Sanders inspired much of the early telemedicine programs in Texas, that ultimately led to Byron Brooks, MD and Oscar Boultinghouse MD sparking the idea that became Teladoc.

Sanders and Michael Gorton wrote #1 Bestselling and Award winning, Digital Medical Home in 2022. Over the years, Sanders and Gorton have become close friends and jokingly call each other "father and son." This is a play on the "Father of Telemedicine" title often given to Doctor Sanders.

Harvey Castro, M.D., MBA served in the U.S. Army, is a veteran emergency physician, bestselling author, and AI futurist shaping the future of healthcare through innovation and technology. He currently serves as Chief Medical AI Officer at Helpp.ai and advises Phantom Space, the Singapore Ministry of Health, and the Texas Medical Association.

A dynamic thought leader, Dr. Castro has delivered four TEDx talks and is the founder of multiple health-tech ventures. With a portfolio of over 30 healthcare apps, he bridges the gap between clinical practice and cutting-edge AI, advocating for ethical, human-centric technology in medicine. His leadership emphasizes empowering both patients and providers through responsible AI integration.

Based in Dallas, Texas, Dr. Castro is widely sought after as a speaker on the intersection of health, technology, and innovation. His work has been featured across national media, and his influence continues to expand globally through education, advisory roles, and writing.

Selected Works by Dr. Harvey Castro:

- ChatGPT and Healthcare: The Key to the New Future of Medicine

- The AI-Driven Entrepreneur

- Success Reinvention

- The Future of Healthcare: AI and Telemedicine

- 2030: A Blueprint for Humanity's Exponential Leap

So many people played significant roles during the years of building Teladoc. For this book, it was necessary to minimize the characters, but I think it worth mentioning that in the beginning, it was just Byron and me. Soon, we were joined by Shannan the website and graphics guru (who came up with the name – Teladoc) Michelle and Derek, who did all the early programming, David who answered the phones, Bruce B, who worked with Roger M to put together the Physicians Association, Shelley who designed the call center app and doctor training. Ruthie stopped the chaos at the door. Gary had huge dreams and marketing skills. Laura and her team made us famous with PR magic. Jeff G and Richard L brought sales across the finish line. Rocky solved the legal problems and always made us laugh! Dan P always wrote the checks when we needed a little boost, and Ken who wrote the first check and delivered it with Deb's cherry pie!

Nathan Morton, founder of CompUSA believed in us from day 1 and helped us through so many trials, before sadly dying. Jerry White, Doctor Bob & Rick B were crucial assets, as was the legend, Carl Dickerson!

No smart CEO goes anywhere without his CFO, and Bill went everywhere with me, often accompanied by Bruce Q, who had the keys to so many doors. Bill and I still work together with companies that are creating innovation and saving the world.

In the later years Noel ran IT and passed that baton to Jeff. I passed my baton to Jason, who did an extraordinary job! Alon brought in a whole new kind of innovation. Cousin Laurel kept the culture and inspiration. Teladoc is now run by a brilliant executive named Chuck alongside an extraordinary Chairman named David S.   I could go on forever, but instead, I will just put some first names. You know who you are! Buzz, Tommy T, Newt, Roger S, Joel R, Grant, Jerry, Tin-Cheun, Bill H, Alice, Amanda, Jessica, Hope, Todd, Alice, Sommer, Mandi, Lisa, Sonya, Patti, Tam, LeeAnn, Bobby, Scott, Meghal, Marsha, Sidney M, Clifford, Patrick, Kevin, Dedrick, Kara, Steve I, Lynn, Elizabeth, Wesley, Dan P, Stacy, Kelly; Carl, Henry D, Joe, Dirk, Dennis, James O, Maria, Kingdon, Steven, Sheran, Fritz, Janet. …hundreds more.

Every book has bad guys. For this odyssey, there were more than I care to mention. Sadly, some were insiders. Life teaches us that, often, the people we trust are the most dangerous in difficult situations. We stayed away from the insider bad guys in this book, though that is perhaps another story. While Benedict Crane and Victor Malor play the villains in this book, they are an amalgamation of many we dealt with, and later, Jason managed as well. The Federal Board is fictitious and plays the role of the 50 State Boards. We had altercations with 17 State Boards during my term, and I helped a doctor with an 18th coming into Covid. I would imagine Jason had his fair share of that as well.

The next step in this journey is incorporating AI into healthcare. Harvey Castro and I are considering a sequel to this book that would cover those adventures!

<u>Other books by Michael Gorton</u>

1. **USSA**, political thriller written in 1994
2. **Lex Talionis**, political thriller and sequel to USSA, written in 1998
3. **Born Again American**, inspirational book, written in 2011 as part of the inspiration for the Shelley Laine song
4. **Forefathers & Founding Fathers**, written in 2016 is a historical fiction from the beginning of colonial America taking place in the early 1600s. This book became a #1 best seller and won several literary awards. Brown Books republished the book in 2017
5. **Broken Handoff**, business book, written with co-authors Seth Gordon and Darien George. The book became a #1 bestseller and named the #1 M&A book of 2019
6. **Digital Medical Home**, written in 2022 with co-author Jay Sanders, MD. The book won awards, and became a #1 best seller. It tells the history of the telemedicine industry.
7. **Tachyon Tunnel 1**, written in 2023 is a science fiction that won awards and became #1 bestseller.
8. **Calamistunity**, written in 2023 is a business book that teaches how to turn calamity and mistakes into opportunity.
9. **Tachyon Tunnel 2**, The Daklin Empire. Science fiction sequel to Tachyon Tunnel. #1 Best Seller, inner of Literary Titan Award, Reader's Favorite 5-Star Book, National Indie Excellence Award, American Bookfest Fiction Award, International Impact Book Award.